PRAISE

Family Money

"The action barrels along to a shocking conclusion . . . Zunker knows how to keep the reader hooked."

—*Publishers Weekly*

An Equal Justice

HARPER LEE PRIZE FOR LEGAL FICTION FINALIST

"A deftly crafted legal thriller of a novel by an author with genuine knack for a reader-engaging narrative storytelling style."

—*Midwest Book Review*

"A gripping thriller with a heart, *An Equal Justice* hits the ground running . . . The chapters flew by, with surprises aplenty and taut writing. A highly recommended read that introduces a lawyer with legs."

—Crime Thriller Hound

"In *An Equal Justice*, author Chad Zunker crafts a riveting legal thriller . . . *An Equal Justice* not only plunges readers into murder and conspiracy involving wealthy power players but also immerses us in the crisis of homelessness in our country."

—*The Big Thrill*

"A thriller with a message. A pleasure to read. Twists I didn't see coming. I read it in one sitting."
—Robert Dugoni, #1 Amazon bestselling author of *My Sister's Grave*

"Taut, suspenseful, and action packed with a hero you can root for, Zunker has hit it out of the park with this one."
—Victor Methos, bestselling author of *The Neon Lawyer*

An Unequal Defense

"In Zunker's solid sequel to 2019's *An Equal Justice*, Zunker . . . sustains a disciplined focus on plot and character. John Grisham fans will appreciate this familiar but effective tale."
—*Publishers Weekly*

Runaway Justice

"[In the] engrossing third mystery featuring attorney David Adams . . . Zunker gives heart and hope to his characters. There are no lulls in this satisfying story of a young runaway in trouble."
—*Publishers Weekly*

NOT
OUR
DAUGHTER

NOT OUR DAUGHTER

A
THRILLER

CHAD ZUNKER

THOMAS & MERCER

Published by Thomas & Mercer, Seattle

www.apub.com

Amazon, the Amazon logo, and Thomas & Mercer are trademarks of Amazon.com, Inc., or its affiliates.

ISBN-13: 9781662516214 (paperback)
ISBN-13: 9781662516092 (digital)

Cover design by Caroline Teagle Johnson
Cover image: © Natalia Lebedinskaia, © MRaust, © Douglas Sacha / Getty

Printed in the United States of America

To Jason & Maggie,
whose real-life story inspired this one

PROLOGUE

The sudden pounding and doorbell ringing at the front door startled him. He glanced over at the clock on his nightstand. Seventeen minutes past midnight. But he wasn't asleep. How could he possibly fall asleep on the worst day of his life? He looked beside him, where his wife lay. She'd taken powerful prescription sleeping pills to knock herself out. This was after they'd spent hours earlier in the day just holding each other and sobbing uncontrollably. The hurt ran so deep. Like nothing he'd experienced his entire life. It felt like someone was reaching inside him and crushing his soul with their merciless hand. At one point, because he couldn't get his wife to calm down, he'd thought he was going to have to make a trip to the ER to have her sedated. Thankfully, that had become unnecessary.

More pounding and incessant ringing of the doorbell. Whoever was out there was clearly not going away. He slid out of bed, pulled on his pajama pants and a gray T-shirt, and then took a quick peek into the crib in the corner of the bedroom. Marcy was fortunately still asleep. The abrupt noise had not stirred her awake. At nine months old, she had been theirs for the past eight months. In every way but birth, she was their daughter, despite the court's cruel decision today. They'd experienced every first with her—first rollover, first solid foods, first crawl, first pull-up at the coffee table. Marcy had even said her first word just this past week: *Da-da*. It had moved him to tears. She just kept saying it repeatedly with the biggest smile on her face. *Da-da! Da-da! Da-da!* But tomorrow morning at ten, she would no longer belong to them. He would no longer be her da-da. The judge had made that decision today in court after leading them to believe, just a month ago, that she would grant them full parental rights. They were absolutely crushed. That word didn't even feel adequate. He wasn't sure his wife would ever recover. After years of infertility issues, tens of thousands of dollars spent on in vitro fertilization, and two horrific miscarriages, they'd believed they finally had their family. They had allowed themselves to fully embrace it the past month.

And then everything was yanked away in a split second.

More pounding and doorbell ringing. He stepped down the hallway of their custom-built five-thousand-square-foot home in an affluent Austin neighborhood, then hustled up to the oversize glass front door. His jaw dropped. Candace. Marcy's biological mother. The person whom the judge had granted full parental rights today. A twenty-one-year-old who'd been messed up on drugs and in and out of jail several times over the past eight months, while they'd been fostering and raising Marcy as their own. She'd somehow miraculously cleaned herself up over the past month and even gotten sober—at least according to a representative from a rehabilitation program who'd testified on her behalf today. He had to admit Marcy's mother had looked like a completely different person in court today. Well dressed and put together. She'd provided proof of new employment as an administrative assistant. She was also a few months pregnant with Marcy's half sister, which seemed to be the real clincher for the court. The judge decided she couldn't split up the sisters. And that was that. Their dream was dead.

But the pretty young woman did not look the same tonight. Her long blond hair was completely disheveled. Eyes bloodshot. Makeup smudged. She wore only a black tank top and red micro shorts. She was barefoot. Why was she here looking like this? Was she back on drugs already? He pulled the front door open. She fell straight into him, knocking him back a bit, before he grabbed her to keep her from landing on the hardwood floor. That's when he realized there was blood all over the front of her. What the hell? The blood was now on his own T-shirt and smeared across his forearms. He eased her down to the floor and turned her over onto her back to see her face. She was gasping. He noticed the midsection of her tank top was torn and completely saturated in blood.

He cursed. Had someone stabbed her? Or shot her?

"Candace, what happened? What's going on?"

She was coughing up more blood. "He's coming!" she cried.

His forehead bunched. "Who's coming? Who did this to you?"

"You have to . . . get . . . out of here!"

She could barely get the words out. Candace suddenly shook violently and then heaved blood straight up into his face. He jerked back, tried to wipe it with his arm, which only made it worse. He looked out his front sidewalk to the street to see if someone was indeed out there. Her white Toyota Corolla was parked out front, driver door open, vehicle still running. But he didn't see anyone else. He needed to call the police. He needed to get an ambulance to the house as fast as possible. She was in jeopardy.

"Please!" she managed. "He's coming here . . . for her!"

His brow furrowed. "For who?"

"Marcy! Get her as far away as possible. Just leave!"

He felt his chest tighten. Someone was coming for Marcy? What was happening?

"But the . . . judge," he said, stammering. "She said . . . she's not our daughter."

"She is . . . now. Save her."

The young woman drifted a second, her eyes rolling back.

He grabbed her shoulders, shook her, his heart racing. "Who's coming, Candace?"

This brought her back for a moment.

"I'm so sorry," she said.

And then she was gone.

ONE

Special Agent Mark Burns was used to people obeying his orders. He'd been with the FBI for more than twenty years, had worked his way up into a prime DC position, and was well respected by nearly everyone. But his teenage daughter, Izzy, was not one of his subordinate agents. She seemed to revel in scoffing at his requests. Burns gave her a lot of grace and didn't push back too much right now. The divorce had been brutal on his fifteen-year-old. Izzy already didn't want to spend her designated days with him. He was careful to not shove her even further away. She'd made it very clear she blamed him for ruining her family. *He lived at the office. He was never around enough. He abandoned Mom all the time for work. Of course her parents had grown apart. It was all his fault.*

Burns still had not told her it was her mother who'd had the affair. He knew it would only further destroy her. And clearly his ex-wife, Nicole, had no intentions of sacrificing herself in this situation by telling their daughter the truth. Even after exposing his wife's cheating, Burns still hadn't wanted the divorce. It was just not the way he was raised. His parents had been married for fifty-four years and counting. They didn't have a perfect marriage, but they'd stuck it out through thick and thin. Burns wanted to put in the counseling work and somehow make it right between them again. But Nicole clearly just wanted out. He figured she wanted to get caught. It had not been a difficult case for him to crack.

"I thought this morning was fun," he said, sitting behind the wheel of his Ford Explorer as he drove Izzy back to her mom's. "Did you?"

Izzy looked over at him with a serious scowl. "The zoo, Dad? Really? That's your idea of fun? Do you think I'm still ten years old?"

"Okay, maybe it was lame. Sorry. But the ice cream was good, right?"

She just rolled her eyes and stared off—a move she'd perfected since the divorce. But Izzy was right. He was definitely out of touch. He hadn't initiated much one-on-one time with her in the years before the marriage blew up, so he was still learning what she thought was fun at fifteen. So far, it seemed to be sitting undisturbed in the second bedroom of the barren condo he'd recently rented and spending hours scrolling through social media until her time with him was up. But he wasn't going to stop trying.

"I keep asking you what you want to do, Izzy," he said, turning down a street into his old neighborhood, where Nicole still lived in their house. "But you never tell me *anything*."

"That's because I don't want to do *anything* with you," she muttered, staring out her window. "Can't you understand that?"

Burns sighed, pulling up to the curb outside a standard two-story redbrick that looked like most of the other houses in this middle-class, suburban neighborhood. They'd moved out of their downtown apartment and into the house when their daughter was only two years old. Burns had wanted Izzy to have a backyard. He'd expected to be there forever. His parents still lived in the same home where he'd grown up, back in Louisiana. He and Nicole had put in a lot of sweat in the early years to make their new place feel like a home. He missed the warmth and comfort of the house. His condo had white walls with nothing on them yet. He barely had any furniture. Probably why Izzy didn't want to spend much time there. But he was still too numb about his marriage imploding to set up a new home.

"Listen, I'll try to think of something better next time," Burns said, putting the car in park. "Have a great rest of your weekend."

Izzy grabbed her duffel bag from the floor, got out, and walked up the front sidewalk to the house without even saying goodbye. Burns slumped in his seat, took a deep breath, and let it out slowly. He kept telling himself things would eventually get better, to just give it more time, but he was starting to doubt it. The distance between him and his daughter was killing him inside. Whether Izzy believed it or not, she really was his whole world.

His phone buzzed. He grabbed it from the cup holder.

Agent Davis. His right-hand man.

"It's my day off," Burns answered. "Hell, it's your day off, too, Davis."

"I know. Sorry, boss. But I thought you'd want me to call about this."

"What's up?"

"Not sure yet. Could be nothing. Could be something. But we just got a ping on a financial account we've been monitoring that's been dormant for over thirteen years."

"What case?"

"Greg and Amy Olsen."

Burns perked up. "You're kidding me?"

"You remember that one?"

"Vividly. Are you at the office?"

"Of course. I can get more done on Saturdays around here."

"I'll be there in twenty minutes."

Davis was waiting for him outside his office when he arrived. Because it was Saturday, his thirty-year-old lead agent was dressed casually in a well-pressed brown polo, designer blue jeans, and white tennis shoes. He looked like he could be in a clothing ad for Abercrombie & Fitch. Davis had been an all-American lacrosse player at Maryland back in college. Tall, with lean muscles, he still looked like he could dominate on the field. Burns was the antithesis of his right-hand man and felt admittedly insecure standing next to him when attractive women were around. He was twenty years older, five inches shorter, and owned a regular dad bod, and his thinning hair was quickly graying on the sides. He hadn't always been this soft. He'd once played baseball at Louisiana Tech. He knew he'd have to get in better shape if he ever wanted to get back into the dating scene. Davis kept urging him to download one of those stupid dating apps. Apparently that's what everyone was doing these days. It was the new normal. But just the thought of it made him want to vomit.

"Nice shorts," Davis said.

"Shut up," he replied. He'd worn a pair of Hawaiian swim trunks and a New Orleans Saints T-shirt to the zoo that morning because there was a ride where they might get wet. But Izzy had shown no interest in going on it.

Burns opened the door and led them inside. The office wasn't much. L-shaped desk, two guest chairs, window view of an adjacent steel and glass structure. The Washington Monument was hidden somewhere on the other side of the building.

Davis handed him a report. "JM Bank, Cayman Islands. Account opened thirteen years, two months, and twenty-seven days ago by someone named Ethan Jones. Deposited one hundred and fifty thousand dollars. Hasn't been touched until this morning."

Burns remembered tagging the account as suspicious because it was opened from the same bank Greg Olsen had been using on the day he'd disappeared—even though he'd never been able to officially tie the two names together. He'd forgotten all about it.

"How much was withdrawn?" Burns asked.

"Every penny, boss. With interest, it was around two hundred and twenty-three thousand."

Burns sat in his leather office chair and started scanning the report. Over $220,000 transferred out after just sitting there for thirteen years. Why?

There was a name listed for who had accessed the account. Cole Shipley. Bank of the West. Fraser, Colorado.

"What do we know about Cole Shipley?" Burns asked.

"Not much, really. We've started looking, but there's not too much out there. He appears to be a teacher at a tiny private school in Tabernash, Colorado. There's a listing with that name in the school directory. But we've found *nothing* on social media."

"Any photos?"

"Just one, in the school directory. I attached it to the back of the report."

Burns flipped to the end and stared at a glossy profile printout of a man who looked to be in his forties with wavy, shoulder-length hair, glasses, and a well-trimmed brown beard. He took in the face for a moment, searching for any resemblance to someone he'd exhaustively hunted more than a decade ago. Greg Olsen had short hair, was clean shaven, didn't wear glasses, and was slightly pudgy. They looked completely different—except for maybe the eyes. He couldn't be sure. It had been so long.

"Any mention online of family or other known associations, clubs, activities?"

"No, boss. It's weird. But then this is small-town America. Tabernash only has, like, six hundred people in it. So my guess is there's probably not a lot of folks around there who post too much on the internet."

"Or maybe he's someone who's covered his tracks for more than a decade."

"Maybe. This was your personal case?"

Burns nodded. "Back when I worked in Austin, a long time ago."

"Yeah, I read the file. Kinda crazy."

"It was. And something that's haunted me for years."

"I bet. You don't lose too often."

"We got an address for this Cole Shipley?"

"Yes, sir—98 Cozen's Pointe Circle, Fraser, Colorado. In the Rocky Mountains, next to Winter Park ski resort. About ninety minutes from Denver."

"I doubt this is anything. But call the Denver office. Have them send someone out there to poke around. Tell them to lie low but try to get some photos and ship them my way."

"Will do."

TWO

Cole Shipley smiled at his wife and teenage daughter, who sat across the picnic table from him. Both were laughing hysterically while sharing a giant blue cotton-candy-flavored ice cream cup covered in pink sprinkles. His daughter had ice cream smeared on her nose, and she was trying to do the same to her mother. But Lisa kept playfully swatting her spoon away. His wife had never looked more attractive to him. She'd aged much more gracefully than he had. Shoulder-length brown hair, green eyes with only a few wrinkles, fit as could be since she ran the mountain trails every day. Although in her forties, Lisa could still easily pass for twenty-nine, in his opinion. Not that he was in bad shape. The trails and ski slopes of Colorado had also been good to him over the years. He was fitter now than when they'd married nearly twenty years ago. It was hard to believe it had been that long. They'd been through so much together. They'd *survived* so much together, was a better way to put it. But today was all about Jade, who was celebrating her fourteenth birthday. In many ways, Jade looked like her mother—long brown hair, bluish-green eyes, bright smile—but none of this came from shared genetics. It had become more difficult to conceal the truth as she grew into a beautiful young woman and kept wanting to compare her facial features to her mom's and dad's.

But they could never tell her. For her own safety.

"Are you sure you don't want some, Dad?" Jade asked, holding out the ice cream.

He laughed. "And risk getting attacked? No, thanks."

"Your loss. It's delicious."

They were sitting next to Miyauchi's Snack Bar, staring out over Grand Lake, Colorado's largest and deepest natural lake. Kids on the sandy beach played in and out of the water. Families were renting Jet Skis and boats at a marina just up the way. Many others were out walking along Lake Avenue and enjoying the shops. It was a beautiful summer Saturday in Colorado. They'd made it an annual tradition to drive over from Winter Park every year on Jade's birthday. It was always lunch at the Historic Rapids Lodge, which sat alongside a flowing water inlet, followed by ice cream at Miyauchi's next to the lake. They'd been doing it for years, and Jade still seemed to enjoy every minute of the experience. He knew that might change as she grew older and became more independent. But he hoped not. He didn't want his little girl to grow up. He always wanted to be nearby to protect her, in more ways than one. He was already having nightmares at the thought of Jade moving away for college in a few years.

"Do you want to rent Jet Skis?" he asked.

Jade scrunched up her face. "Not this year. My back is kind of hurting today."

He nodded, pressing his lips together. For the past few months, every time his daughter said something like that, it felt like a dagger to his heart. But that was going to change starting today. "Everything will be better soon. I promise."

She tilted her head. "How?"

He'd been waiting all day to share this exciting news.

"We're finally going to be able to move forward with the surgery. I'm calling the doctor first thing on Monday morning to get it scheduled."

Jade smiled wide. "Really?"

He matched her smile. "Yes, really. Happy birthday, sweetheart."

Jade immediately slid off the bench, came around the table, and hugged him tightly. Cole noticed Lisa tilt her head at him with narrowed eyes, but she didn't say anything in the moment. He knew that discussion was coming. Jade had been a competitive cheerleader for years. From an early age, she could tumble and do back tucks with ease. She'd quickly become a star at their local gymnastics gym. But she also had a severe case of scoliosis. It wasn't obvious with her clothes on. She could hide it well—other than when she wanted to wear a bikini on the lake. Despite their ongoing efforts to deter it, the curve in her spine had gotten much worse this past year as she hit a serious growth spurt. With that growth had come major discomfort. There were nights when his daughter could barely fall asleep because she was in so much pain. It had caused her to pull out of cheer a few months ago.

They'd met with a specialist, who'd recommended spinal fusion surgery. The surgeon felt like he could get her back up and going again, pain-free, in a couple of months. But because they had crappy health insurance, they hadn't been able to schedule the surgery yet. It'd been horrible watching his daughter deal with not only the physical pain but the emotional anguish that came with stepping away from her love of cheer. So Cole had done what he had to do this morning to rectify the situation.

All smiles, Jade bounced away from the picnic table to go to the restroom.

Alone, Lisa gave him another stare. "You accessed the account?"

He nodded. "This morning. What choice do we have, Lisa? Just sit here and let our daughter suffer? I'm done waiting on the insurance company. They may never approve it."

"Yeah. It's just . . . risky."

"We talked about this last week. You said it was ultimately my decision."

He'd grappled with the decision every second of every day for the past week.

"I know. It just stirs up the emotions."

"I really do think we're safe by now. Besides, did you see the look on her face? That was the happiest I've seen her in months."

Lisa looked over toward the restroom. "You're right. She *really* needs this. So much of her joy is wrapped up in her cheer life. Just scares me, that's all."

"Eventually, we must stop living in fear—and just live. It's been over thirteen years."

"That's easier said than done."

Jade returned. They got up and walked down a path by the water and up to the beach. Jade and Lisa both took their sandals off, stepped into the sand, and moved down to the water. Their sundresses allowed them to wade in without getting their clothes wet. Cole watched them hold hands as they moved into the lake up to their knees. He knew the water was freezing cold. They were both making faces that told him it was nearly insufferable. But they were also laughing about it. He took a moment to fully take in the two of them. His girls. He would do anything for them. He would sacrifice everything for them. He already had. And no matter how overwhelmingly challenging that was, he hadn't regretted it for a single moment.

A child squealing loudly across the way grabbed his attention. Cole turned around. A little boy was not happy about his snack and was letting his mom know all about it. Then something else caught Cole's attention, just to the left of the crying child. There was a man holding a camera with a long lens positioned slightly behind a cluster of trees. The guy looked out of place wearing black slacks, a white long-sleeved button-down, and black dress shoes. He was probably in his early thirties, with close-cropped brown hair. Cole squinted. Was the camera lens pointed straight at him? He took a quick glance around, trying to see if there were others who might have the guy's attention. But there was no one. When Cole turned back, the guy was already walking away down the sidewalk. Cole watched him for a moment. About ten steps down, the guy stopped again and aimed the camera out toward the water. Then he kept on walking, stopping to grab more shots here and there.

Cole exhaled, not even realizing until that moment he'd been holding his breath. It was just some random guy. Cole had just told Lisa they had to stop living in fear. But was it even possible? For most of his adult life, he'd been watching over his shoulder. And he had to admit that accessing the account today had put him slightly on edge. He had no way of knowing if anyone had ever connected him with the offshore accounts. He'd created two accounts under two different names on the day they left Austin. Eight years ago, he'd tapped into one of the accounts when they'd needed money to buy their current house. Nothing came of that. No one showed up at their door flashing badges. And now they were several more years down the road. Were they even really looking for them anymore? He kept watchful eyes on the guy with the camera until the man finally walked around a building and disappeared entirely.

It was probably nothing.

THREE

Agent Burns sat in a battered leather recliner—recently purchased at a garage sale—in front of a cheap, forty-two-inch flat-screen TV in the living room of his otherwise empty condo. He was watching *Raiders of the Lost Ark*, even though he'd seen the movie a dozen times already. He had nothing else to do this afternoon but watch Harrison Ford outrun a massive boulder. Saturdays had really sucked since the divorce went final. He often found himself bored as hell, ready for the weekend to quickly pass so he could just get back to the office already. In his pre-divorce life, he usually spent weekends working in the garage on various projects—or outside, taking care of the yard. He loved the smell of fresh-cut grass. But he had neither a garage nor a yard in this condo building. To make matters worse, his ex-wife was letting their yard go to hell. She was probably doing it to spite him. He'd buy a house for himself again one day. But divorce was expensive, so that wasn't in his current budget.

He stood up, walked over to a window in the living room, and peeked through the blinds. The sun was beginning its descent behind the ugly apartment building right next to his. Weekend nights usually stank even worse than the days. He was lonely. Perhaps he should hit up a bar somewhere. Although he wasn't even sure where to go these days—he hadn't done the bar thing in years. There was a pub right around the corner, but the thought of going there all by himself made him feel like a real loser. He considered calling Agent Davis, seeing if the guy wanted to hang out since he'd made the offer here and there. But Davis probably had hot dates every weekend night. Burns had a few buddies his age who were also divorced, but all they seemed to do was sit around drinking heavily and badmouthing their ex-wives. He'd rather do that by himself.

He grabbed his phone, typed out a quick text to his daughter.

Batting cages at Cameron Run tonight? Chocolate shakes after?

He knew it was a long shot. Especially after the disaster this morning at the zoo. But he'd overheard Izzy mumble to a friend on the phone earlier that she had no plans tonight. If she wanted to go with him, surely Nicole would allow it, even if it was off schedule. They used to go to Cameron Run a lot as a family. A place with a water park, minigolf, and batting cages. How long ago was that? Five years? Would Izzy also now consider this place lame? Did anyone ever outgrow hitting baseballs and drinking shakes?

He stared at his phone screen and perked up when he noticed the dots suddenly appear, showing his daughter was actually replying to his text. But then the dots disappeared just as quickly without any message showing up. He watched for a few more seconds, but nothing happened. Izzy had clearly gotten his message but had chosen to ignore him. He sighed, set his phone down, walked over to the fridge, and grabbed a bottle of Guinness. It was looking like beer and Chinese takeout again. Then his phone started ringing. He hurried back over, hopeful. He frowned when he saw Agent Davis's name on the screen.

"What?" he answered with a grunt.

"Hey, boss. This is a bad time?"

"Yeah, kinda busy," he lied. "But I got a moment."

"Good. Check your email. I just sent you a digital package."

"What's in it?"

"Photographs from Colorado today. Cole Shipley. They just arrived from our guy in Denver. I'm having them run through facial recognition, but I thought I'd go ahead and send them over to you."

"All right, give me a sec."

Burns sat at his small wooden kitchen table, opened his laptop, and logged in to a secure server. The email from Davis sat at the top of his inbox. He accessed the attached file and watched as a dozen high-resolution photos populated on his screen. The first couple of images were of the same fortysomething guy who was listed as a teacher on the private school website, sans the eyeglasses. He stood alone by a lake or something. Burns searched his laptop and opened an old file that contained all the information on the Greg and Amy Olsen case. He hadn't been inside this folder in years. He enlarged a photo of Greg and Amy together at a park somewhere that the FBI had seized from their home during the investigation. They were in their early thirties in the photo. Burns did a quick comparison between the two men. Maybe a slight resemblance but it felt inconclusive. While Greg Olsen had been a bit pudgy with short hair and clean shaven, Cole Shipley looked to be in excellent shape, with long hair and a full beard.

He scrolled through the rest of the photos. Cole Shipley was sitting at an outdoor table with what looked like a teenage girl and a woman. Burns's eyes locked in on the woman, and he immediately leaned forward. He enhanced the image, and then he cursed out loud. Amy Olsen. She looked slightly different from thirteen years ago. Brown hair instead of her previous blond. But there was no mistaking it was the same woman. The face was a dead giveaway. When you are as attractive as Amy Olsen, it's nearly impossible to hide it, no matter what measures you take. This had to be her.

He jumped out of his chair, cursed again, even louder.

"What is it?" Davis asked.

Burns felt his adrenaline racing. "Where were these taken?"

"Grand Lake, Colorado. The woman has been identified as Lisa Shipley. She helps coach cheer part-time at a local gym. The girl is their daughter, Jade Shipley."

"We got an age for the daughter?"

"Yes. Today is apparently her fourteenth birthday. They were celebrating."

Burns did quick math in his head. Same age as Marcy, the baby they'd taken.

He'd found them. He'd *finally* found them.

"You think it's them, boss?" Davis asked.

"I *know* it's them."

Now Davis cursed excitedly. "What do you want me to do? Have Denver grab them?"

"No! Get us on a plane ASAP. I need to be there. I don't want anyone screwing this up. Tell our Denver guy to not let Cole Shipley out of his sight, even for a moment."

"Will do. This is huge!"

"I know. I'll meet you at the airport shortly."

Burns hung up, sat there for a moment, stunned. He went back to the old digital file on Greg and Amy Olsen. It had been more than thirteen years since they'd murdered Candace McGee inside their home and then disappeared with her baby in the middle of the night. A child they'd fostered to adopt for eight months—until the judge had made the decision to return the baby to her mother. Family and friends had told Burns and his team in the aftermath how absolutely devastated both Greg and Amy had been on the afternoon of that fateful decision. Their motive was very clear. Although Greg Olsen had deleted all security camera footage, they didn't need it. They'd found the murder weapon inside the house: a seven-inch petite chef's knife that matched a set in the kitchen. It was covered in Candace McGee's blood *and* had Greg's fingerprints on it. A neighbor had discovered the body by looking through the glass front door midmorning the next day when she came over to check on them.

Burns had no idea how long the Olsens had been gone. An analysis of timelines gave them up to a twelve-hour head start. But he knew they had fled north, at least initially. The FBI found their Lexus SUV abandoned in a Target parking lot in Waco later that afternoon, where

Burns discovered they'd also withdrawn ten thousand in cash from a bank. But that was the very last sign of them.

Their life on the run had undoubtedly been helped by Greg Olsen's previous career. After graduating with honors from Arizona State, Greg had quickly worked his way up the corporate ladder, eventually heading up the security and fraud division of a large international banking system. His job was literally to protect the bank from stolen and fake identity hacks. Greg knew that world inside and out and had made contacts all over the globe. Burns eventually tracked down an individual who worked underground in Prague who admitted he'd helped Greg get new identities the day after they'd disappeared. The man claimed he knew nothing about the crime—he was on the other side of the world. They were just business acquaintances. He'd created fake identities for Greg Olsen on many occasions over the years to test against the bank's security operations.

Burns had searched long and hard for the first three years after they'd disappeared. Twice, he thought they actually had them. Once in Casper, Wyoming. A year later in Boise, Idaho. But both raids had ended in failure. Burns had lost support from the top after the last disaster. Resources for his search eventually dried up. He was told if the Olsens somehow fell into his lap again, he could ratchet up the pursuit. Until then, he was to get busy solving other crimes. The whole thing had been a big F on his FBI report card.

Burns stared at the photographs from Grand Lake. Greg and Amy looked happy sitting there, eating ice cream, enjoying life as Cole and Lisa Shipley. He wondered how long they'd been living under the new names. He'd concluded years ago they'd likely left the country and probably settled somewhere in South America or Europe. But Colorado? This was a surprise. He studied the teenage girl. Jade Shipley had to be Marcy McGee. But there was obviously no way of telling by simply comparing photographs.

He checked his watch. Within five hours, he was going to have his first actual conversation with the fugitive couple. It was hard to believe. He hurried to his bedroom, threw together a quick overnight bag, and then bolted for the door.

FOUR

The Fisk & Whitmore Law Firm occupied the entire fifteenth floor of a newly built trophy office building in the heart of Washington, DC. While the firm, with only eighty-two lawyers, wasn't the biggest in DC, Fisk & Whitmore had been a political powerhouse for more than thirty years. At sixty-six years old, Carl Fisk had represented some of the most influential political figures going all the way back to the beginning of the Clinton administration. Fisk's massive office had a sweeping view of the Capitol. He would often stand at the expansive floor-to-ceiling windows and stare out over the Capitol grounds, as if overseeing his kingdom. Which was how many in town viewed him: the king of the hill. If you were a major player in town and had a serious legal issue, you called the king. You also privately called the king when it was not just legal but scandalous.

Fisk was good at fixing things, inside and outside the court of law.

He currently stood at his office window wearing a standard dark-blue business suit, a neatly pressed white button-down, red tie, and gold cuff links given to him by George W. Bush. The suit jacket hung from an antique coatrack behind his desk. Fisk wore an expensive custom-made suit every day of the week—mainly because he was in the office every day. The only time you'd catch him not impeccably dressed was while sleeping or while rowing in the Potomac, which he'd been doing since

Harvard. The exercise had kept him in great shape over the years. He could pass for midfifties if not for the silver hair, which he didn't mind. It made him look more distinguished. While this wasn't Hollywood, looks still meant a hell of a lot in this town. Image was everything.

He took a sip from his glass of Macallan and stared out over the bright lights of the most powerful city in the world. It had been a stressful day. He just wanted to enjoy his scotch and try to take the edge off.

There was a knock on his door, followed by his assistant poking her head inside. Like him, Brenda worked nearly every day. She'd been with him for twenty-six years. She probably knew more DC political secrets than the entirety of the Senate. And he paid her twice as much as their government salaries.

"Sir, Mr. Lester is here."

"Okay, you can let him in."

Ross Lester had been a friend and confidant for more than two decades. A valuable friend, since he worked inside the elite inner circles of the FBI. A balding, pudgy guy nearing sixty, Lester entered the office wearing a cheap brown suit and holding a briefcase. He'd always reminded Fisk more of a community college professor than an intelligence expert.

"You really need to get better suits, Ross," Fisk said.

"You've been telling me that for years."

"I'm reminded of it every time you come see me."

"Not all of us have our own tailor, Carl. Some of us work in the real world."

"That's a shame." Fisk offered a hand toward a sitting area with a long black leather sofa and two leather chairs. "Have a seat. You want a drink?"

Lester sat on the sofa and shook his head. "Nah, can't."

"If you knew the expense of what I'm holding in my hand, my friend, you would never turn it down. Believe me."

"Yeah, well, Nancy has been riding my ass lately about my drinking. I can't afford to have that on my breath when I get home, no matter the cost."

"Again, a shame."

Fisk walked back over to his bar, poured himself another glass.

"Well, what's so urgent?" he asked Lester, who had texted him only a few minutes ago.

"I got an unexpected hit on one of the cases you've had me monitoring."

Fisk had Lester keeping tabs on dozens of cases that were all directly or indirectly connected to his multitude of clients. In return, he'd treated Lester to many of the city's luxuries over the years. The best seats at ballets, shows, sporting events, and restaurants. Lester once said Fisk was the only reason his marriage to Nancy had lasted. She loved to be treated to the good life. Something the FBI could never afford them.

"Which one?" Fisk asked.

Lester popped open his briefcase, pulled out a manila folder. "Something that has been cold for a long time. Greg and Amy Olsen ring a bell?"

It took some serious restraint for Fisk to keep from spitting out his whisky. Those were the last two names he wanted mentioned around him right now.

"What kind of hit?"

"They found them."

This time Fisk felt a tremble move through him and he dropped his glass. It shattered on the hardwood floor. He quickly tried to calm himself, but his hands were shaking.

"You all right?" Lester asked.

"Yeah," Fisk managed, swallowing. "Damn thing just slipped out of my hand."

He didn't bother with the glass shards; instead, he quickly stepped back over to Lester.

"Where are they?" he asked.

"Colorado, apparently."

"How did they find them?"

"A wire transfer from an offshore bank."

"Have they already apprehended them?"

Lester shook his head. "No, not yet. We're headed that way right now."

"Who is?"

"Mark Burns. This was originally his case."

"Are they sure it's them?"

Lester handed him the folder. Fisk flipped it open, again trying to hide the fact that his hands were jittery. There were a dozen color photographs inside. A man standing by himself by a lake and then sitting with a woman and a girl.

Lester said, "Seventy percent computer match on the guy. Ninety percent on the woman. But Agent Burns is *one hundred percent* certain it's them."

Fisk quietly cursed, glanced over toward five flat-screen TVs mounted on a wall behind a small conference table. Each was tuned to political news. All the stations were currently showing clips from today's confirmation hearings for the newly nominated candidate for the US Supreme Court. The hearings in front of the Senate Judiciary Committee had been a bloodbath the past three days. He was exhausted.

"How much time do I have?" he asked Lester.

"What do you mean?"

"How much time until they take them into custody?"

Lester shrugged. "Probably four hours. Burns wants to be there himself."

Fisk could feel sweat building up on his lower back and under his armpits.

"You don't look so good," Lester mentioned. "You sure you're okay?"

"Yes, I'm fine. Can I keep these?"

"Sure. Just make sure they don't get out."

"Of course. All right, I gotta get back to work."

Lester stood, headed for the door. "My wife has been dying to eat at that new sushi place that just opened over on Pennsylvania Avenue. Nakashimi. But it's booked out for two months. Anything you can do?"

Fisk's eyes remained glued to the photographs. "Tell Brenda on the way out. She'll make it happen."

"Appreciate it."

Fisk looked up. "Hey, Ross."

The man turned around.

"Keep me posted on this situation. Anything and everything you know. No matter the time of day or night. It's that important to me. I need you to be my eyes and ears."

"Of course."

Fisk watched the man step out of the office. Lester knew better than to ask any details about how Fisk could possibly be involved. That had been part of their deal for decades. No questions. Just information. Alone again, Fisk rushed back over to his desk, careful to not step on the broken glass, and grabbed his cell phone. His contact answered immediately.

"You alone?" Fisk asked.

"Yeah, in my hotel suite. Why?"

"We've got a *serious* problem."

FIVE

Brock Gunner had been running the massive ranch for more than fifteen years. At over 520,000 acres, it was the third biggest in Texas. But he'd been working for the family for more than twenty-five years. That's what everyone in West Texas called them—*the* family—because they were such a powerful force in these parts. He'd started with them as a sixteen-year-old high school dropout ranch hand and worked his ass off sunup to sundown, gaining the respect and trust of most everyone around. But it took him killing a man who'd betrayed the family in a bad oil deal for the patriarch to bring him into his inner circle. Brock was twenty-two when he'd pulled that first trigger, burying the body where no one would ever find it. That's when his status really grew. He soon became an enforcer for the family. At six foot two and built like a linebacker, he was damn good at it. When the family had an issue, Brock would step in and resolve it. That usually meant breaking bones or such to get their point across. But there had been other times when more drastic action was required.

He knew this was one of those times.

Brock was sitting in his black Ford F-450 Super Duty truck with a digital tablet in his hands. There was nothing but blackness outside all around him. No light from a house or another vehicle for miles. He could see every star in the sky. There was nothing quite like it. He'd lived in Odessa proper for a few years but always hated it. Couldn't see the sky like out here on the ranch. But right now his face was glued to the bright tablet screen, which cast a glow over his thick beard. An encrypted file had just been emailed to him. He typed in the necessary password, and the file opened. There were numerous digital photos inside, along with a document that contained names, addresses, and other pertinent information.

Brock picked up his phone, texted: I'm inside the file.

He received an immediate response: Good. The plane should be there any minute.

He studied the photographs. A man probably slightly older than him with a woman and a teenage girl.

He texted: All of them are targets?

Brock had killed a kid once before. But that was a drug-dealing teenage boy who had tried to carjack him outside a bar late at night. He'd had no choice. That skinny kid had a jittery trigger finger. This was different. But protecting the family at all costs was his life's purpose. If it weren't for the family, he'd probably be in prison right now—or in the grave. He stared back down at a close-up image of the girl. It was hard to believe she was the one who'd indirectly started this whole mess thirteen years ago. Although Brock had never met the people in the photographs, he shared a deep and dark connection with them. After all, he was the reason they'd been running and hiding all these years.

Brock sent another text: How much time will I have?

Not much. Feds are already in route. You'll probably arrive just before them. Get in and out without anyone noticing.

They have people already on the ground?

Just one. You'll have to somehow deal with him.

What about cops?

They haven't brought in the police yet.

Good.

Brock, everything is on the line for us right now. Take care of this.

I understand. He looked up through his windshield and spotted lights approaching in the sky at a distance. He texted: Plane is here.

All right, keep me updated every step of the way.

Copy that.

Brock put his phone away and grabbed a small duffel bag of clothes he'd quickly thrown together when he first got the call fifteen minutes earlier. Hopefully he wouldn't need a change of attire. If everything went as planned, he'd be back at the ranch sometime after midnight. But the bag also contained a small arsenal. He would certainly need that. He also grabbed a long black rifle bag. After getting out of the truck, he circled to the front bumper. He wore blue jeans, cowboy boots, a white T-shirt, and a brown, wool-lined, waxed trucker jacket. Rows of bright lights suddenly appeared on the ground beside him, revealing a long airstrip. He watched as a private plane slowly descended. The airstrip was something the family had built many years ago. The plane touched down, hit the brakes, then eased to a stop right in front of his truck. The jet engines stayed running. It was a beautiful Gulfstream G600. Brock knew nothing about private planes, but he'd searched it up when he found out the family had spent more than $50 million. Brock had been on it several times already when the family had wanted him to travel with them for security reasons. He always felt out of place amid the luxury of it all. He'd usually tried to at least clean the cow crap off his boots on previous trips. But he didn't have time for that tonight.

The door opened and the stairs popped out. A pilot stood at the top. Brock trotted over, bounded up the stairs.

"Hey, Justin," he said to the pilot. "How you doing?"

"Been better. Was at my kid's baseball game when I got the call."

"Sorry about that."

"It's the job, man. Why the hell are we going to Granby, Colorado?" The pilot glanced down at the rifle bag. "You going hunting?"

Brock smirked, thinking about how he might be using the gun.

"Something like that."

SIX

Lisa Shipley heard a sudden scream come from upstairs. Jade. It jolted her. There was real terror in her daughter's voice. She dropped the wooden spatula she was using to stir up chocolate icing for the birthday cake she'd just made, then hustled around the corner to the stairwell. Their house was a small two-story in a nice neighborhood. It sat on a street of similar homes in a valley squeezed right in between the towns of Fraser and Winter Park. There were only two bedrooms upstairs. One was set up with gym mats covering the floor and a mirrored wall where Jade practiced her cheer jumps. For years Lisa and Cole had listened to constant *thuds* coming from upstairs because their daughter would be up late practicing. The other was Jade's bedroom. Could someone be up there with her daughter? Had Lisa been so busy in the kitchen she didn't hear an intruder enter the house? She'd regularly had that very nightmare for the past thirteen years. Someone sneaking in and taking Jade in the middle of the night. She would often wake up drenched in sweat and gasping for breath. She doubted the bad dreams would ever go away.

Another shriek, followed by, "Mom!"

Lisa rushed up the hardwood steps, nearly slipping as she reached the top because she was wearing only socks. The screaming was coming from Jade's bedroom. When Lisa got there, she found her daughter standing on her bed with a look of horror on her face. Lisa scanned the room but didn't see anyone else.

"Jade!" Lisa said. "What's wrong?"

Jade had one hand covering her mouth. With the other, she pointed to the floor near the entry to her bathroom. Lisa turned, squinted, searching, and then spotted a two-inch scorpion scuttling its way across the floor. She let out a deep exhale and felt relief pour through her. It was just a stupid bug—or technically an arachnid. Not an intruder. Good grief. The screaming was about a scorpion. Not someone trying to abduct her daughter.

"Seriously, Jade?" Lisa said, rolling her eyes. "You dang near gave me a heart attack!"

"Just get rid of it, Mom! Please!"

Lisa picked up a tennis shoe from the floor near Jade's desk, walked over to the scorpion, and gave it a good whack. It took a second smack of the shoe to get the job done. Then she grabbed tissue from the bathroom, picked up the smushed scorpion, and flushed it down the toilet. When she exited the bathroom, Jade was still up on the bed.

"You can come down now, dear," Lisa said, laughing. "The beast is dead."

"Check the floor again," Jade insisted. "There could be more. I heard they travel in pairs."

"Where did you hear that nonsense?"

"YouTube."

"YouTube? Really? Get your silly butt down from there."

Jade timidly got off the bed, still looking all around. She was wearing the pink and white pajamas they'd given her earlier for her birthday. She had a white exfoliating mask smeared on her face, though she barely needed it. Her skin was nearly flawless. Lisa had battled acne issues when she was Jade's age. But then they weren't from the same genetic pool. That had become more difficult to dance around as Jade got older. Her daughter had often mentioned how she didn't think she looked like either of her parents. Living a lie with your own child felt like betrayal.

Lisa hated it. She didn't want to do it anymore. But Cole continued to remind her that it was the only way for them to truly protect her. The more Jade knew, the more dangerous it became for her—and all of them. Maybe one day, when she was an adult. Maybe never. They just didn't know yet. *One day at a time* had been their mantra with Jade from the beginning.

"I don't know how you do that, Mom," Jade exclaimed.

"Do what?"

"Calmly walk over there and smash that thing, like it's no big deal. How do you not freak out? Those things are hideous and dangerous. And they gross me out."

"Well, honey, you're going to have to overcome a lot of fear to make it in this world."

Her daughter had no idea just how much fear her mother had had to overcome just to be standing in the same room with her right now. Lisa had faced hell itself and lived to see the other side. Compared to that, scorpions were easy.

"You *always* tell me that," Jade said. "But I'm only fourteen. I'm not ready to take on scorpions yet. Maybe when I'm fifteen."

They both laughed at this comment.

"Those pajamas look great on you," Lisa mentioned.

"I love them. They are *so* soft and comfortable."

"Good." Lisa smiled. "So have you had a good birthday?"

Jade's perfect smile stretched ear to ear. "The best birthday ever. Especially because you let me go hang out with Tyler this afternoon."

Tyler was a fifteen-year-old boy from school. They'd been texting nonstop for weeks.

"You really like him, don't you?"

She nodded. "But don't tell Dad. He gets so crazy when I mention boys."

"I know. It kills him. But cut your dad some slack. You're his baby."

"He's not living in reality, Mom. I'm growing up. Where did he go, anyway? I heard his truck drive off a few minutes ago."

"Grocery store to pick up vanilla ice cream. He knows you love it with your cake."

"I do! Chocolate cake and vanilla ice cream are my favorite."

"Well, get your face washed up. Your dad will be back soon."

Lisa stepped toward the bedroom door but then stopped and turned around. Jade was already in her bathroom, splashing water from the sink on her face and cleaning off the skin mask. Lisa stood there and watched her for a moment. It was hard to believe her daughter was fourteen today. Each birthday had felt like such a miracle. They'd been through so much to get to a place where they could watch Jade grow up like a normal child. For years, Lisa had lived in fear that they wouldn't see her next birthday. Or the next. That they'd finally be discovered and Jade would be ripped from their family. But things had really stabilized for them in Colorado. Life was basically normal here.

Well, as normal as it could get when they were still on the FBI's most wanted list.

SEVEN

Cole pulled his gray 1998 Dodge Ram pickup into a parking spot outside the Safeway grocery store near his home. Shifting into park, he turned the key and listened to the struggling engine sputter and cough for several seconds before finally shutting down. It did the same thing when starting up. The disturbing noises had grown worse over the past month. He wasn't sure how much longer the truck would survive without putting in a whole new engine—which probably wasn't worth it on a vehicle with more than 250,000 miles on it. He'd purchased the pickup with cash when they'd first moved to Colorado. It had been a trusted ride for a long time. He just wanted it to hang in there for a little while longer. Every extra dime they had needed to be reserved for Jade's surgery expenses—although accessing the offshore account had helped with that stress.

His cell phone buzzed. A text message from Lisa.

Can you also pick me up a tub of cookies & cream? ☺

He responded with a thumbs-up and smiled. This had been a good day. He hadn't felt this content in a long time. He'd loved spending so much time with Jade on her birthday. Quality time had been harder to find lately as she became more independent. She was always off with friends now. But she at least still seemed to enjoy hanging out with her parents. His teaching job put him around young adults and their families all the time. He knew teenagers wanting to spend any time with their parents was an anomaly. Maybe he and Lisa could somehow sidestep the moody-teenager-hates-her-parents stage. He laughed to himself. Unlikely. He knew it was coming. Especially when he started enforcing stricter boundaries around the whole "boy" thing—as if he didn't know where Jade had sneaked off to this afternoon. Tyler seemed like a good kid. But even good kids couldn't be trusted. Cole knew he'd have to keep close tabs on that situation. Lisa seemed to have forgotten how they'd behaved when they first started dating back in high school.

It was difficult to believe that had been more than twenty-five years ago. Their courtship began as juniors, when they paired up in science lab. He fell for her almost instantly—the eyes, the smile. But it was mostly her calming demeanor. Cole could be controlled by his big emotions. Sometimes too high, sometimes too low. But Lisa had a way of steadying the ship inside him. After high school, they'd both headed to Arizona State. They were never apart. Lisa was all he knew—and all he ever wanted to know. They got married right after college graduation. That was an incredible day with lots of friends and family. His older brother was his best man. Her two younger sisters were her maids of honor. His mom cried. Her dad even shed tears. Cole sighed just thinking about it. All people they loved so dearly whom they hadn't seen or spoken to since the night they'd disappeared.

That had been the most brutal part of their thirteen-year journey. They could never risk contacting family. They'd learned that the hard way their second year on the run, when Lisa had called her mother from an old pay phone at a random convenience store. Four hours later, the police had shown up at their apartment building. The Feds clearly had her parents' phones tapped. Fortunately, Cole and Lisa weren't at their apartment at the time. A neighbor had texted Lisa and asked why the cops were banging on their apartment door. She said there were four police cars in the parking lot with lights swirling. Cole wasn't sure how the FBI had tracked them to the apartment so quickly. But they hit the highway with Jade within minutes of that text message and never looked back.

Lisa had made the phone call to her mother that day only after monitoring social media channels and finding out her father had gotten very sick and was in the hospital fighting for his life. Unfortunately, her dad passed away, and when he was put to rest a week later, Lisa wasn't there. She didn't get a chance to say goodbye. She didn't get to hug on her sisters or mourn with her mother. She'd cried herself to sleep for two weeks straight afterward. It was a gut-wrenching experience. One of many they'd endured.

Cole got out of his truck and headed toward the front doors of the grocery store. He rubbed his arms. It was a crisp night, and he wore only a Denver Nuggets T-shirt and blue jeans. He should've grabbed a light jacket or hoodie. The parking lot was about a third full. Mostly trucks and SUVs. If you didn't want to slip and slide in the winter, you'd better have four-wheel drive. The snow could dump fast and heavy. You might not be able to get out of your own neighborhood some days without it.

Cole stepped out of the way as a black Ford Taurus pulled up his row and slowly passed by him. He gave a casual glance at the driver and then paused to give a quick look back. The driver looked oddly familiar. Was it the same guy who'd been over in Grand Lake taking photographs earlier today? He watched for a moment as the driver parked five spots over from his truck. But he didn't get out right away. What was he doing? It didn't look like he was on his phone or anything. He was just sitting there. Cole squinted but couldn't tell for sure if it was the same guy, so he turned and continued into the store.

He grabbed a small grocery basket near the front and navigated back to the frozen dessert section. He found a tub of Jade's favorite vanilla ice cream, then a tub for Lisa, and began heading toward the front. When he turned the corner of an aisle, he stopped, stepped back. The guy from the parking lot had entered the store and now stood across the way near the front. Cole quickly backtracked. Then he peered around the end of the aisle again. It was definitely the same guy. Cole had never seen him before today. Was it only a coincidence he was there inside this store with him right now? Perhaps. These were small towns. You tended to run into the same people all the time.

But this man didn't seem local. He was wearing the same clothes he'd had on earlier: white button-down, black dress pants, black dress shoes. If he was local, wouldn't the guy have gone home to change into something more casual? It had been more than eight hours since they were at Grand Lake. He was just standing there, his eyes intently bouncing all around, as though he were searching for someone. Cole wondered if that someone could be him. Had the guy actually been taking photographs of him earlier? If so, why? This didn't sit well with Cole. He'd become an expert over the years at monitoring those who gave him second looks or stared at him a bit too long. He was always paranoid the next stranger he encountered could be the one to destroy his family. Maybe it was nothing. But he needed to figure this guy out fast, or at minimum it would leave him unsettled and ruin the rest of his night.

Cole set his grocery basket down and briskly walked in the opposite direction, away from the guy. He couldn't go straight out the front doors. From the guy's current position, he would be able to see that. Instead, Cole found a swinging door in the back of the store where employees entered and exited. He pushed through the door, nodded confidently at a store worker, whose eyes narrowed while looking up at him, and kept on moving—like he belonged back there. He entered a stockroom with huge metal shelves filled with various boxes and wooden crates. He quickly shuffled through that area until he spotted a massive, open garage door, as well as a cargo truck currently being unloaded. Hurrying over in that direction, he stepped around some of the workers, then hit a set of concrete steps outside. Safely on the pavement, he took off running, swiftly circling around the outside of the grocery store, until he was finally up to the front again.

Peering around the building's corner, Cole made sure the guy in the black slacks was not standing directly out front. There was no sign of him anywhere, so Cole rushed into the parking lot, staying close to the edge, tucked out of view, then finally came in from the back of the cars. Cole hesitantly approached the black Ford Taurus, making sure he didn't miss someone else who may have also been inside the vehicle. The car sat empty. He leaned into the passenger window. There was a Starbucks cup in the cup holder. A name was scribbled with a black marker. Todd? He now had a first name. There was a pack of cigarettes in the middle console, along with a package of wintergreen gum. Sitting in the front passenger seat was an accordion folder of sorts with rubber bands around it. He couldn't find anything written on the outside of the folder.

He tried to open the car door, but it was locked. He moved to the back window. A couple of fast-food bags lay wadded up on the floor. One was for a chain they didn't have in Winter Park. A black duffel bag sat in the back seat, unzipped, but Cole couldn't see what was inside it. He quickly circled the vehicle and peered in from the opposite back window. That's when he felt a level of panic hit his chest he hadn't felt in more than ten years. It nearly dropped him to his knees. A feeling he'd hoped to never experience again. But it was here, nevertheless. A dark-blue jacket was folded up in the back seat, and he could clearly see three familiar, bold yellow letters emblazoned on the back. FBI.

EIGHT

Agent Burns sat in the front passenger seat of a black Chevrolet Tahoe as it sped away from Denver International Airport and headed toward the mountains on its way out to Winter Park. GPS said it was an hour-and-a-half drive. He'd instructed his local driver to get there in half that time. They had a red, swirling police light up on their dashboard, letting others on the road know their speedy zigzagging was official business. The red light was bright against the backdrop of night. His fingers felt jittery with anticipation. A thirteen-year pursuit was about to finally come to an end. Three FBI agents rode in the vehicle with him: Agent Davis and two others from his DC team who'd traveled with them. Like him, they all wore standard dark-blue FBI jackets. Ready for action as soon as they arrived. Another six local FBI agents were behind them in a matching Tahoe—also racing down I-70.

Burns felt like ten FBI agents should be plenty to make the arrest. This was only one man, his wife, and their teenage child. They weren't a gang of criminals. While Greg and Amy Olsen had certainly committed a violent crime thirteen years ago in the stabbing death of Candace McGee, there had been no other official reports of violence from them in the days and weeks after that event. The couple had not gone on a killing spree to aid their escape. Burns had determined McGee's death was a crime of passion from two overly distraught individuals who'd momentarily lost sanity. Of course, he took nothing for granted. The couple could lose control once again when they suddenly felt cornered.

He studied a digital map of Winter Park on his iPad. There was a pin placement for their home address, and he'd noted four different exits in and out of the neighborhood. If all hell broke loose, they would need to cover them all. He swiped his screen left and once again examined the surveillance photos of the couple they'd captured earlier that day. The FBI's tech team said Cole and Lisa Shipley didn't exist before ten years ago. They just suddenly appeared in Colorado—undoubtedly from Greg Olsen's expert hands. Burns wondered how many different identities they'd used in the years directly after their disappearance. Both had official driver's licenses, according to the Colorado Department of Transportation. But there was no record of US passports. The couple didn't have plans to travel outside the United States. Or they had fake passports under other aliases. Burns was still working on getting access to all their financial accounts.

He looked out the window. They'd exited the main highway a few minutes ago and were now driving on Highway 40, where they'd started the climb up the mountain. The city of Winter Park was nestled in the Fraser Valley on the other side. The permanent population was around a thousand people. But with the ski resort, that could easily triple, depending on the season.

"How much longer?" Burns impatiently asked the driver.

"About thirty minutes. Just gotta go up and down the pass, and then we'll be there."

Burns checked his watch. That would put them there by 9:45. Every minute felt like an hour right now. He heard Davis pick up a phone call in the seat behind him.

"Yeah, let me put you on speakerphone," Davis said, then leaned forward to the front. "Sir, this is Agent Haskins, our local guy who's been trailing Cole Shipley all afternoon."

"What is it, Haskins?" Burns asked.

"I think we've got a problem here."

"What problem?" he barked, not wanting to hear that right now.

"Sir, I believe Cole Shipley is onto me. He, uh—"

"Spit it out already!"

"Well, sir, I followed him into a grocery store a few minutes ago. But then I couldn't find him anywhere. I think he intentionally ditched me. Because when I went back out to the parking lot, his truck was already gone. Not only that, but my back tire was flat. I think he somehow let the air out."

"You're kidding." Burns cursed. "Where are you now?"

"Just changed the tire, about to drive back over to their residence."

"Get there ASAP. And do not let him out of your sight again. You understand me?"

"Yes, sir."

"I'm serious, Haskins. I'll have your ass. This will be the end of your career."

"I understand."

Burns hung up, cursed again. This was so damn bad.

He turned to the driver. "Can't you go any faster?"

"Not without flying off the mountain, sir. These switchbacks are hell."

Davis spoke up from the back seat. "We need to call in backup, boss. We can't chance it. If he suspects he's found, they'll immediately bolt. They've done it before."

Burns checked his watch again. He'd originally wanted to handle this whole matter on their own without involving any local police. In his experience, small-town police could really muck up an investigation. They were too loud and obvious. They were not trained like the FBI for this type of covert situation. But Davis was right. If Cole Shipley knew he was being followed, an escape plan was no doubt already in motion. These were not dumb people. Quite the contrary. He'd found them to be incredibly smart. They could be gone in minutes. Burns could not allow them to get any kind of jump start. He had no choice right now. He needed as many local cops as possible surrounding the Shipleys' house before it was too late. He turned back to Davis.

"All right, call local police. Get them moving!"

NINE

Cole pushed his old truck to the limit while racing home. The tires squealed at every sharp turn, and the vehicle's whole body rattled, as if it might come apart at any moment. He was grateful the truck had started right up in the grocery store parking lot. Every second mattered. At this point, he had no idea how many Feds were already in town. Was the FBI agent alone? Was he still trying to figure out if Cole was the man formerly known as Greg Olsen? Or had that match already been confirmed with the photographs he'd taken earlier, and now the FBI agent was just awaiting the cavalry? Cole had to plan for the latter. They could take no chances. But how had they been found? It had to have been the money transfer from the offshore account that morning. There was no other possible explanation on how the Feds had shown up on his doorstep only hours later. He cursed. He'd rolled the dice and lost. And it might cost them everything.

Their two-story home was a quick drive from the grocery store in the back of a neighborhood called Grand Park. He hoped he'd just bought himself an extra five to ten minutes by jabbing a screwdriver into the FBI agent's back tire. He pressed the gas pedal all the way down, his heart hammering inside his chest. His whole world felt like it was spinning. This was an out-of-body experience. His fingers were numb and shaking as he tried to clutch the steering wheel. He always knew there was a chance they'd be found. They stayed ready. But as the years had turned into a full decade, Cole had started to believe they might be in the clear. He certainly knew Lisa felt that way. They had both been dead wrong.

He dreaded telling Lisa it was time to immediately abandon their whole lives—again. Ten years just wiped away in a single moment. And on Jade's birthday, no less. That reality punched him even harder in the gut. Jade had been only four years old the last time they'd had to pick up and leave. She was easy to fool back then. It was a fun adventure. They'd had plenty of car games and a bagful of her favorite snacks ready. She didn't remember much about it to this day. But this was entirely different. They had no choice but to introduce her to a frightening new reality: her parents were both wanted fugitives. There was no way to predict how she would respond, but she needed to trust them and go willingly.

Any other response from her could be disastrous.

Cole skidded around a last turn and sped down his street. He let out a quick sigh of relief when he spotted his house up ahead with no other cars parked out front. He'd feared the Feds might already be there taking his family into custody. He slammed on his brakes and parked on the street. He didn't even want to waste time in the driveway. He planned to take off immediately after telling Lisa the brutal news. He jumped out of the truck and sprinted up to the front door. He scrambled for his keys in his pocket, quickly unlocked the front door, and stepped inside. He stopped, took a deep breath. He resisted the urge to yell out his wife's name, knowing it would only set the whole house into panic. He needed to do this as calmly as possible in order to also keep Lisa calm.

Before heading to the kitchen, he stepped into his small study and opened the bottom right drawer of his office desk. Inside, he grabbed two cell phones. They were burner phones he kept replacing each year for this exact moment. They would need to ditch their current phones to make sure they weren't being tracked. He could hear noise coming from around the corner. He took another deep breath, let it out slowly, and circled back to the kitchen, where Lisa stood over a chocolate cake. She was busy sticking colorful birthday candles into the chocolate icing and didn't notice him at first. His wife was smiling and humming a happy song. It sounded like U2's "Beautiful Day." He felt sick to his stomach. It might be a long time before she smiled like this again— maybe ever. It crushed him.

She turned, spotted him standing there. Her smile grew even bigger.

"Hey, didn't hear you come inside. Where's the ice cream?"

He swallowed, stepped toward her. Her brow bunched at the sight of his tight face. He could tell she immediately knew something was wrong. He could never hide anything.

"What is it, Cole?" she said, suddenly alert.

But she knew. He could see it in her widening eyes.

"We have to go, Lisa," he said, his voice shaky. "Right now."

"What are you saying?" she whispered, barely getting the words out.

"It's time. They're here. They found us."

She dropped the pack of candles she was holding to the hardwood floor and put her hand to her mouth. "How do you know?"

She was getting wobbly, so he reached out with both hands to hold her up.

"Someone was following me inside the grocery store. I spotted him earlier today over at Grand Lake. And then I found FBI credentials in his car."

"Cole, please, no. Are they on their way here now?"

"I presume so. Which is why we have to go."

"But Jade . . . !" she said. "It's her birthday."

"Listen to me, Lisa," he said, his voice steadier. "We can't focus on that right now. Where is your phone?"

She turned, grabbed her cell phone from the counter behind her. He took it from her and handed her one of the new burner phones.

"Everything is already programmed. Get Jade's phone when you go upstairs and then destroy it. Use the hammer in the kitchen drawer. You understand?"

She nodded. "How much time do you think we have?"

"Five minutes, at most. Just get her out of this house."

"What are you going to do?"

"Ensure you get away from here clean."

She frowned. "How?"

"By leaving first. Making sure they follow."

"Do we go straight to the unit?"

"No. Text me when you're in the clear here and then wait for me across the street at the top of Rendezvous, where we like to park and hike. But leave without me if I don't show or you don't hear back from me within twenty minutes."

Her mouth dropped, her voice rising. "I can't leave without you, Cole!"

"Yes, you can. For Jade. You can do this without me."

"What do I even tell her?"

They had not planned out that part. They'd never wanted to think about the possibility.

"Whatever it takes to get her out of this house."

She again nodded. The color had returned to her face. Her eyes were more firmly set. She was pulling it together. That was good. This was the Lisa he needed right now. This was the Lisa who helped them get away the first time. Brave. Fierce. Determined. For a moment, they just stood there and stared at each other, both probably feeling the exact same thing. This could be the very last time they were together. If he got arrested, they might never see each other again. He thought of Jade upstairs. He didn't even have time to go up and see her. The weight of that was nearly unbearable.

"I love you," she said.

"I love you, too. See you in a few minutes."

"I hope so."

"You will. I promise."

With that, Cole spun around and raced for the front door.

TEN

Lisa watched Cole shut the front door behind him, and then she exhaled so heavily she thought she might pass out. She'd feigned bravery in front of her husband, so he wouldn't worry, but the truth was she was frightened out of her mind. This couldn't be real. This couldn't be happening. She felt completely numb. It had been ten years. A lifetime. Plus, this was different from the past. Back then, they had never really set up a new life. They were too scared all the time to even allow themselves to make new friends or find genuine community. So it was much easier to pick up and just go without word to anyone. But they had a real life here. A life she'd grown to love—at least, as much as she could under the circumstances. It had certainly been difficult dealing with so many financial challenges. Back in Austin, they'd lived an affluent lifestyle. Money had never been an issue for them. Not only did Cole have a terrific job with a high salary, but she was also doing well as a Realtor and making a name for herself. She loved helping people find the perfect home. But neither of them felt like they could pursue opportunities here in Winter Park that might put them in the spotlight. They just couldn't risk it. Cole had especially felt stifled by that choice. He had always been an ambitious guy, so constantly pumping the brakes on career possibilities had gradually stolen a part of his soul.

But they did it all for Jade. Their daughter was not going to understand any of this. It would be devastating to rip her out of her life with no explanation—especially on her birthday. But Lisa had no choice. One way or another, her daughter's life as she knew it was over. She checked her watch, marking the exact time. Four minutes.

She turned, rushed up the stairs. She took several breaths, trying to stay in control. It was difficult. The growing panic felt like a roaring lion inside her. She knew she couldn't allow the wild animal to get to the surface. Not with what she had to accomplish with Jade in such a short amount of time. She'd prayed for years that she would never have to do this. That she would never have to step into her daughter's bedroom and destroy everything Jade thought she knew about her life. But that moment had come anyway. Still, she prayed again, and then entered Jade's bedroom. Her daughter was curled up on her bed, back against the pillows, headphones over her ears, eyes glued to her phone. Probably texting with friends. Just like she did every other free moment. Those days were about to be over. Jade turned toward the door when she finally noticed her mom.

She took off her headphones. "Hey, is Dad home? I heard his truck. But then it sounded like he just drove off again or something."

Lisa swallowed, ignored the question, spoke in an urgent tone. "Honey, listen to me very carefully. We must leave the house *right now*. You have four minutes to throw whatever you can into a bag. And then we're driving away."

Jade tilted her head. "What? Is this some kind of fun birthday thing?"

"No, this is very serious. I can't explain right now. But I need you to do what I just said. We're pulling out of the driveway in exactly four minutes."

Jade's face bunched up. "Mom, what are you talking about? You're kinda scaring me. What's wrong?"

"We're in trouble, baby. Real trouble. People are coming here."

"What? What people? What happened?"

She couldn't stay calm any longer. "Jade, please! Now get moving!"

Her daughter suddenly scrambled out of the bed. "But . . . what am I supposed to pack? Where are we going?"

"Whatever is valuable to you. Nothing more. Don't worry about your clothes."

"What do you mean, don't worry about clothes?"

"I already have a bag of clothes packed for you."

"What? You do? Why?"

"Give me your phone," Lisa demanded, again ignoring Jade's question.

"Why, Mom? You're freaking me out so bad!"

"Please just give it to me."

Jade reluctantly handed over her phone. "I don't understand what's happening!"

Lisa could see tears forming in her daughter's eyes. She pulled Jade into her chest with both arms. "I'm sorry, baby. I know this is so confusing, and scary. But I just need you to trust me right now, okay? Trust your mom. Meet me downstairs. Please hurry!"

Lisa turned, rushed out of the bedroom, bounded down the stairs. She passed through their primary bedroom and into the main closet, where she quickly changed out of her pajama pants and into a pair of blue jeans. She was already wearing a blue sweatshirt with ASPEN stitched in white on the front from a family road trip they'd taken the previous year. She sat on a stool, tugged on socks, and then quickly laced up a pair of Nike running shoes. Then she bolted out of the bedroom and back into the kitchen. She could hear rumbling around from Jade's bedroom upstairs. Hopefully that meant her daughter was doing as she was told. Lisa pulled open a kitchen drawer and grabbed a hammer. She put Jade's cell phone on the counter and banged it hard with the tool. The screen shattered. Several more swings with the hammer and the phone completely broke apart.

Lisa darted from the kitchen, moved into the foyer, and peeked out a front window. She spotted car headlights coming in her direction.

She stiffened, was about to scream for Jade, but then realized it was just their neighbor, Joe Henderson. He passed their home and pulled into a garage two houses down. She gave a quick thought to her neighbors. Their worlds were going to be rocked, too, when they found out the truth about who they'd been living next to all these years. She could hear them now in the days ahead, sitting in camping chairs in the Peters' driveway across the street, while the kids all played outside—like they'd been doing for years—talking about the shock of all this.

They were living right next to us.

We had Cole and Lisa in our home all the time.

Our daughter has been best friends with Jade since second grade.

How could Cole and I fish together nearly every Saturday morning without me knowing anything about any of this?

Lisa was so lovely. I can't believe they committed a murder.

And so on and so forth. Lisa would have no opportunity to ever tell them the truth. To convince them all of it was lies. That hurt her so much. She cared deeply about these people. They had become family. Her only family. And now it would all be shattered. Tears hit her own eyes. She quickly wiped them away, raced back to the stairs.

"Jade! Now! We have to go! Right now!"

Her daughter appeared at the top of the stairs with a black backpack over her shoulder. She'd also changed into blue jeans, tennis shoes, and a Taylor Swift sweatshirt.

"Mom, I'm shaking *so much*. You have to tell me what's going on!"

"I will. But not now. Come on!"

Jade hurried down the stairs. Lisa ushered her daughter forward, through the kitchen, and toward the garage. Jade paused a moment to look down at her smashed-up phone.

"Mom, my phone—"

"You'll get a new phone soon."

Lisa snagged her purse from a counter in the mudroom, grabbed her car keys from a hook on the wall. She hit the garage door opener as they stepped into the garage. She could now hear police sirens not too far off. She stood still a second, listening. It sounded like multiple sirens. Could the police be going after Cole right now? Were they coming to the house? Or was it possibly unrelated to their situation? She felt her new burner phone buzz in her back jean pocket and quickly pulled it out. Her heart dropped. The text message from Cole answered her question and sent a chill straight through her. She swiftly dropped into the front seat of her green Subaru Outback.

Jade got into the passenger seat. "Mom, is that the police?"

"Yes," Lisa admitted, starting the car.

"Are they coming here?"

"Yes, baby. Hold on!"

Lisa shifted into reverse and punched the gas down. The Subaru's tires squealed on the concrete, rocketing backward, throwing her daughter forward into the dashboard. The car sped in reverse all the way into the street, where Lisa yanked the wheel to the right. The quickest way out of the neighborhood was behind her. But that was also, most likely, the way the police were approaching their house. So she decided to take one of the back ways out. Thinking quickly, Lisa pressed the garage door opener on her visor, sending the garage door toward the concrete, hoping it might delay the police a few extra minutes if they thought they were still inside the house. She punched the gas again.

At the next street, Lisa tugged the wheel left, causing the tires to spin like crazy on the asphalt. She then stopped and took one final peek back at their home. A place where they'd created so many family memories. The only home Jade had ever really known. When she hit the gas again, she knew it would be gone from their lives forever. Along with everything inside it. More tears hit her cheeks. The police were now on their street. Multiple vehicles. An army. Lisa pressed the gas down, said another prayer, and sped forward.

God, please help us!

ELEVEN

Five minutes earlier

Cole's eyes were locked on his rearview mirror. He'd had to wait inside his truck for only two minutes before he'd noticed the same black Ford Taurus from the grocery store pull onto his street and settle along the curb a few houses down. Then Cole had calmly driven off, making sure he was followed. He had to do whatever it took to get Lisa and Jade away from the house—even if it meant risking his own freedom. He wasn't sure what to expect. Did the FBI agent suspect Cole had intentionally flattened his back tire? If so, would the guy immediately pull him over? Or was the agent still in watch mode only?

Cole was ready to punch down the gas pedal and go on a high-speed chase. But nothing happened. The agent trailed at a safe distance. Cole exhaled. It appeared he was still only under surveillance. Which was good. He desperately wanted Lisa and Jade to have a drama-free getaway. Of course, he knew a lot of the drama would depend on how his daughter handled the shocking news they were leaving town—forever.

Cole drove the speed limit down Main Street, which was lined with various restaurants, retail stores, shopping centers, and ski- and bike-rental establishments. It was a summer Saturday night, so Winter Park was still hopping with energy. As he got closer to the center of town, he noticed cars parked up and down both sides of the street in every available parking spot. He remembered there was a concert going on at the outdoor amphitheater in Hideaway Park. He rolled down his window and could hear the music pumping. Old-school classic rock. People were out on the sidewalks in droves, carrying camping chairs and packing beer coolers. Cole hadn't been sure up to this point how he was going to evade the FBI agent, but seeing the concert crowd gave him an idea. He pulled into the parking lot of an Italian restaurant called Volario's and parked his truck. A quick peek over his shoulder showed the black Taurus also entering the parking lot behind him.

Cole checked his watch. If all went well at home, Lisa and Jade should be leaving the house soon. He kept hoping to get the text from her that they were in the clear. But nothing yet. He got out of his truck and began casually walking with another group of people toward Hideaway Park. The music was really jamming now. He paused with the rest of the group to allow traffic to clear on Main Street. As he did, he cast another quick glance behind him. The FBI agent was also out of his car, on the move, and headed in his direction. Perfect. Cole walked across the street with the other concertgoers, hopped up on a park path, and navigated his way through a playground and skate park area until he reached the hillside amphitheater on the other side. The crowd grew thick. Probably more than a thousand people.

It was time to get himself lost. He began to briskly weave in and out of the crowd, ducking low at times, zigzagging back and forth. He snagged a black baseball cap he spotted sitting in someone's unattended camping chair, tugged it on his head, and pulled it down low. Cole was halfway through the concertgoers when he suddenly stopped in his tracks. A uniformed police officer stood just ahead of him at twenty feet, arms crossed, monitoring the people and not the stage. Maybe thirty years old. Tall and muscular. Mustache. Cole quickly spun around when the officer glanced over in his direction. The sight of a cop jarred him. While the officer was likely simply working security for the concert, Cole didn't want to be anywhere near the police right now.

He quickly cut a different path away from the officer and walked even faster, threading the crowd.

The summer concert series was a popular event in these parts. People drove in from all the neighboring towns. His own family had been regular attendees over the years. The band members up on the stage looked to all be in their fifties. But they were rocking out like they were still in their twenties. And people in the crowd were hooting, hollering, drinking heavily, and singing along. Cole hurried around them, making his way across the grass hill, before stopping and looking back. His eyes bounced across the hundreds of faces directly behind him. He didn't spot the FBI agent anywhere. Had he already lost him?

He kept going, pushing all the way through the remainder of the crowd, until he reached a sidewalk on the amphitheater's other side. Then he began circling the sidewalk around the outside of the park, trying to quickly make his way back to his truck before the FBI agent decided to return to his own vehicle. If Cole got there first, he'd have a clean getaway. Hands in pockets, he tried to walk as casually as possible along the crowded sidewalk, even though everything inside him wanted to make a dead sprint for it. But that would only draw unwanted attention. The band finished a song, everyone cheered, and then the lead singer started talking to the crowd about something silly, when a sudden loud wailing noise off to the left made everyone turn and stare back toward Main Street.

Cole stopped, stiffened. Police sirens. Several of them, all going off at once, as if the police were beginning to put on their own special concert. Cole knew the Fraser Winter Park Police Station was only a couple of blocks up the road from the city park. The sirens were now drawing closer. Could they possibly be coming for him? Had the FBI agent called for reinforcements? Was the whole block about to be surrounded by police?

He started to frantically look around for his best escape. But then the police vehicles—all black-and-white four-wheel-drive Tahoes—raced past the park without stopping. He counted. One. Two. Three.

Four. Five of them. Probably the entire police force. He cursed. They clearly weren't coming for him. Which meant they were headed somewhere else. That thought sent panic straight through him. He had to presume the worst. He pulled out his burner phone. Still no text from his wife. He quickly typed out his own message: Get out now! Police are coming! He stared at his phone screen, hoping to get an immediate reply from Lisa. But nothing. Then his focus was drawn away from the phone by someone shouting his name directly up the sidewalk ahead of him. And it wasn't a friendly shout.

"Stop right there, Mr. Shipley! Don't move!"

Cole looked up, froze. Thirty feet ahead of him was the same uniformed police officer he'd spotted earlier. In one hand, the cop held his phone, and his eyes bounced back and forth between Cole and the device. Was he looking at a photo of Cole? In his other hand, the officer held out his gun and pointed it in his direction. Other startled people walking next to Cole also froze on the sidewalk. The cop had called him directly by name. Which meant the FBI must've sent something out to local enforcement. Every police officer in the area probably had his photo right now. Things had just escalated. The officer, now talking into his shoulder radio, began a slow walk toward him. Cole was at a decision point. Did he stay put and deal with the ramifications? Or did he risk being shot and run like hell? He doubted the officer would pull the trigger with so many people around. And staying put pretty much guaranteed he'd never see his family again.

Cole chose the latter, spun around, and took off running.

He ducked his head low, just in case. As expected, he heard no gunfire. But he did hear the cop cursing loudly for him to stop while chasing after him. Cole raced across a side street, up onto another sidewalk, and began to cut a path behind the Winter Park Visitor Center and other adjacent buildings. Spotting a narrow alley between two buildings up ahead, Cole took a right at full speed. When he did, his running shoe caught a serious pothole and sent him flying face-first onto the pavement. His ball cap flew off, and he felt his chin hit the surface as he skidded to a stop. He quickly pushed himself up, took a big step forward, and then his left knee buckled on him. This sent him straight to the ground again, where he landed hard on both knees. He'd suffered a knee injury on the soccer team back in high school, and every once in a while, it still randomly acted up on him.

But this was the absolute worst timing possible.

He again pushed himself up and tried to take off running, but it was too late. The cop tackled him from behind. Cole went down with the officer on top of him. He tried to fight back, but the cop was stronger. He stopped resisting altogether when the officer stuck his gun so forcefully into Cole's back he thought it might puncture the skin beneath his T-shirt.

"Don't move, or I will be forced to fire my weapon," the cop said, panting. "This is my final warning to you. Do you understand?"

Cole nodded, grunted. "I understand."

He again thought about Lisa and Jade. Had they made it out? Were they gone from the house by the time the police arrived? Or had they also been apprehended? Would he and Lisa be separated from Jade and never even get the opportunity to tell her the truth? Would their daughter grow up from here actually believing her parents had murdered her biological mother to take her for their own? That was the story that had been perpetuated in the national media for all these years. Cole felt despair push in on him like a devastating avalanche. It was over. At least, for him. Cole heard the officer call in the arrest on his radio.

"Suspect in custody . . . requesting immediate backup . . . alley next to Deno's—"

Then Cole heard a sudden loud *thump!* The officer made a deathly gasp, then immediately went silent and collapsed right on top of him. What had just happened? Cole pivoted on the pavement, looked back, and spotted a stocky guy with a full beard standing over him with his own gun in his hand. It looked like there was a gunfire suppressor of some sort attached to his weapon. He was probably in his early forties. Blue jeans, cowboy boots, brown trucker jacket. Cole squinted and noticed a small black symbol tattooed on the back of the guy's gun hand. He stared at his face and couldn't believe his own eyes. Although it had been thirteen years, he clearly recognized him. How could he not? The very same face had haunted his dreams for more than a decade.

The bearded guy flipped the limp officer over with the toe of his boot. Then he aimed his gun directly at the cop's forehead and fired another muffled round. *Thump!* Cole winced at the horrific sight and felt blood and other tissue splatter across his face. Something told Cole he would be the next victim if he didn't react immediately. So when the bearded guy turned to take aim at him, Cole kicked his right foot up as suddenly and forcefully as he possibly could, like he was doing a scissor-kick with a soccer ball. His shoe hit squarely on the guy's gun hand, dislodging the weapon and sending it flying across the alley.

The killer cursed, spun around, went after his gun. When he did, Cole got up and began wildly scrambling out of the short alley, keeping his head low. Although his knee still hurt, he had no choice but to push through the pain. He heard another *thump!* and felt his left arm jerk forward, like someone had just punched him as hard as they could in his tricep. Had he been shot? There was no time to stop and check. He heard yet another *thump!* as he hit the sidewalk out in front of Deno's Mountain Bistro and slid around the corner. This time, he didn't feel anything. There were groups of people out on the sidewalk. Cole swerved back and forth, hoping to avoid more gunfire. While he'd doubted the police officer would risk shooting into a crowd, Cole didn't think this guy played by the same rules. As fast as he could, Cole hobbled back toward the concert venue and quickly got himself lost inside the massive crowd again. He circled back and forth for several minutes before finally making his way out the back and pressing himself up against the brick wall of a restroom facility.

He was out of breath and sweating profusely. He looked down at his left arm and could see blood dripping from his elbow. He examined the spot more closely and found a bloody gash on the outer part of his tricep. He had definitely been shot, which was surreal. But it looked like the bullet had just grazed the outside of his arm, and while his arm stung, it didn't hurt too badly. Maybe his adrenaline was numbing the pain. Cole peeked around the corner, searched the faces. Had the stocky guy pursued him all the way into the crowd? He didn't currently spot him anywhere. And he certainly wasn't going to wait around long enough to find out. He thought about his truck. He couldn't go back to it. The FBI agent or the police would be camped there. He couldn't even risk a taxi right now.

He felt his phone vibrate in his pocket, quickly pulled it out. Lisa. Finally.

We're safe and waiting. Where are you?

Cole felt relief pour through him. Rendezvous, a community of mountainside homes and cabins, was only a mile away. He wondered if he could do the climb on foot considering his wobbly knee. But he had no other choice right now.

He quickly typed a reply.

Be there in ten minutes.

And then he took off running again.

TWELVE

Cole fought for breath as he made his final ascent up a street called Pioneer Trail to the top of Rendezvous Mountain, where his family should be waiting for him. Because he'd so aggressively attacked each winding road, his legs felt like they were on fire. The running had been difficult on his knee, but it had held up okay. He was almost there. Thankfully the streets were dark, and it was easy for him to pass by homes without being noticed. He wondered if the police had posted anything about him on social media. He didn't want to have to deal with some old man trying to make a citizen's arrest right now.

Halfway up the mountain, Cole began to hear police vehicles swarm the city block around the concert below. Word was probably out that a police officer had been shot and killed. It was a horrible thing to witness firsthand and would be a devastating blow for this small town. But Cole couldn't stop wondering if the police would think he'd pulled the trigger. After all, the last thing the officer had said on his radio was that Cole was in his custody. Had anyone seen the stocky guy go in or out of the alley? Would someone be able to verify Cole was innocent of the crime? He couldn't get the stocky man's face out of his mind. It was shocking to see him after all this time. Who the hell was the guy?

That was a question he'd been asking himself for more than thirteen years. A question he'd never come close to answering, no matter how much time he'd spent searching the internet and trying to sort it all out. He still had no clue. What was the guy suddenly doing here in Winter Park? How had he shown up in the alley out of nowhere? Had he also been following Cole around? Could the guy somehow be working with the Feds? That seemed highly unlikely considering he'd just shot and killed a police officer. But why had the guy done it? Did he not want Cole arrested?

None of it made sense.

Just like none of it had made sense thirteen years ago.

He couldn't waste energy thinking about it right now. He needed to place all his focus on getting his family out of town as quickly as possible.

He followed one last switchback neighborhood road and finally spotted Lisa's Subaru Outback parked along the curb up ahead of him. There was a trailhead near this spot where they would often go hiking. They could see all of Winter Park from up here. Lisa and Jade stood next to the vehicle watching what was happening in the valley below them. They were clearly fixated on the wild scene at Hideaway Park and didn't notice him at first. Cole had no idea what Lisa had already communicated to Jade. He wasn't sure what kind of response he was going to get from his daughter. Was she furious at him? Thankfully, when his daughter turned and noticed him, she ran toward her dad and threw her arms around him.

"Daddy, I'm so scared," she said. "The police are at our house right now."

"I know, baby," he said, holding her tightly. "I'm scared, too."

"Mom won't tell me *anything*. She said I had to wait for you."

"We'll explain everything soon. I promise. But right now, we have to go quickly."

Lisa came over to their circle and hugged them both. He wrapped his arms around his whole family, his whole life, and felt momentarily relieved, considering just a few minutes ago he hadn't been sure he'd have this opportunity again. He could see the shock written all over his wife. Pale face. Wide eyes. Trembling hands.

"You okay?" he asked her.

"I don't even know how to answer that right now." Then she squinted at his face and touched his cheek with her fingers. "Cole, is that blood?"

He'd forgotten all about having the police officer's blood and tissue splattered across his face. He quickly grabbed the bottom of his T-shirt and wiped it off.

"It's nothing," he insisted.

"Dad, what happened to your arm? It's really bleeding."

"I fell. That's all. I'll be okay."

Lisa pitched her head, clearly not believing a word of it. But he subtly shook her off, like a pitcher with a catcher—as if to say, *Not now, later.* She didn't push him.

"Everyone in the car. Right now. We have to go."

Lisa quickly got into the front passenger seat; Jade climbed into the back. Cole turned around, took one last look down at the town. There seemed to be blue and red blinking lights nearly everywhere. Police vehicles, ambulances, fire engines. Around the park and on the street where they lived. It was a surreal scene. They'd left their home with basically nothing. Every physical part of the life they'd built for themselves over the past ten years was still inside. Photos, office files, financial statements, mementos, Jade's cheer trophies and ribbons—*everything.* It would probably all be destroyed as the FBI searched every square inch of the place. But the Feds would find nothing connecting them to where they were going next. He always stayed prepared for that. It was all part of the plan.

He sighed. The plan. He'd hated having to have a plan all these years.

But he needed the plan more than ever now.

He took another deep breath and let it out slowly, recognizing the finality of the moment.

Cole and Lisa Shipley, and their daughter, Jade, were officially dead. They no longer existed. It was time to become someone new.

THIRTEEN

As their black Tahoe finally pulled onto the Shipleys' street, Agent Burns stared at a row of red and blue blinking lights parked along the curb outside their fugitives' home. Two uniformed police officers stood guard at the front door, while a couple of other officers milled about on the sidewalk. There were no signs of any arrests. No suspects locked in the back of police vehicles or handcuffed out on the front lawn. No urgency at all. On the contrary, the officers all looked quite dispirited, like they'd just been sucker punched or something. What the hell was going on?

The drive through the mountain pass a moment ago had been hell on Burns's cell phone signal. He'd lost a full ten minutes—which felt like an absolute eternity right now. Haskins, their man on the ground, wasn't answering his phone, and neither were any of their local police contacts. Because of that, Burns hadn't received any updates about the situation here in Winter Park, and he was losing his mind. Especially after driving through town a few seconds ago and taking in a chaotic scene with a flood of police activity. He had a bad feeling it was all connected to their pursuit of Cole and Lisa Shipley.

The Tahoe's driver parked in the driveway, and the second Tahoe pulled in beside it. Everyone quickly got out. Burns and Davis huddled on the front sidewalk.

"This doesn't look promising at all," Davis said, hands on hips.

"No, it sure as hell doesn't."

At that moment a thirtysomething guy with close-cropped brown hair, wearing the same dark-blue FBI jacket as Burns and the others, stepped out of the house and hustled down the sidewalk toward them.

"Agent Haskins," he said, introducing himself upon arrival.

They all quickly shook hands.

"Why haven't you been answering your damn phone?" Burns asked, irritated.

"Sorry, sir. I lost it in pursuit a few minutes ago."

"Pursuit where?"

He nodded to his right. "The concert midtown. All hell has broken loose over there."

"We noticed," Davis said. "Give us the quick rundown."

"I followed Cole Shipley from this house. He drove directly into town and got out on foot at the park. Then he took off into the concert crowd. I pursued but couldn't keep track of him. There were way too many people around." Haskins blew out forcefully, shook his head. "But then maybe I got lucky. Not so much for the cop."

"What about a cop?" Burns asked, brow bunched.

"You guys haven't heard?"

"We just got here, Haskins!" Davis blurted. "What the hell are you talking about?"

Haskins ran a hand through his hair, exhaled again. "Shipley shot and killed a police officer a few minutes ago. Apparently, after you put the word out here, a local officer spotted him at the concert and managed to apprehend him in an alley two blocks away. I didn't see any of it. But somehow Shipley shot him dead before fleeing again."

Burns cursed. "So he's still on the run?"

"Yes, sir."

"What about his wife and daughter?" Davis asked.

"I don't know. I believe they were here when I left to follow Shipley. But police officers said no one was at the house when they arrived.

However, all the lights were left on inside and a water faucet was still running upstairs. They must have barely missed them."

Burns put two and two together. "He probably lured you away from here to give his wife a clean getaway. I presume there is no car in the garage?"

"Correct. But they couldn't have gotten too far."

Burns glanced across the street, where a collection of neighbors had gathered to take in the scene. "You talked with any of them?"

"Not yet. But I was planning on it."

"This is a nightmare," Burns grunted, shaking his head. "What's the last known location for Shipley?"

"The concert venue."

"So he could still be hiding in that crowd?"

"Yes, sir. Police are trying to break it up. But it's a zoo."

Burns turned to Davis. "Get over to town ASAP with the rest of the team. See what you can find. Tell Simmons and Myers to stay here with me. We'll begin working forensics."

"Yes, sir. Come with me, Haskins."

Davis rushed off to rally the others.

Burns rubbed his face in his hands, still not believing that Cole Shipley had shot and killed a police officer. It certainly didn't fit the profile he'd created. He wondered how it had even gone down. Did Cole have a gun on him? Did the officer not immediately disarm him? Or had Cole somehow taken the officer's own weapon away and then used it against him? That was a difficult maneuver even for a skilled military man—which Cole was not. Something didn't feel right about it. He needed more information.

A white truck with huge mud tires sped down the street toward the house and skidded to a stop directly in front of Burns. He watched as a heavyset, gray-bearded man wearing a cowboy hat, a black Fraser Winter Park Police jacket, blue jeans, and brown boots got out. The older man stomped right over to him, looking none too pleased.

"You Burns?" he barked.

"Special Agent Mark Burns."

"Lee Jackson, chief of police."

Burns offered a hand, but Jackson ignored it. The man's face was flashing red, and the veins in his forehead bulged.

"You have no idea how badly I want to take a swing at you right now, Burns," he said through clenched teeth, his fists noticeably balled.

"I don't understand, Chief."

"How the hell could you not tell me a dangerous fugitive was living in my town?"

"Well, we didn't know until earlier this afternoon."

"And yet you still waited several hours to inform me. You didn't trust us until it was too late. And because of that, one of my officers is dead. Shot down in cold blood by your fugitive. And that really pisses me off."

"I just heard that news. It's tragic."

"It's more than tragic. Tommy wasn't just one of my officers—he was also my damn nephew. Kid used to ride around with me in my police truck all the time when he was young. All Tommy ever wanted was to be like his uncle." Jackson swallowed, fighting back his emotions. "Hell, he has a young wife and twin boys at home."

Burns grimaced. That personal note punched him hard in the gut and brought on a fresh wave of guilt. He'd made the call to wait to apprehend Cole Shipley. And now two boys would go a lifetime without their father. "Look, I'm sorry, Chief. My sincere condolences. We obviously never intended to put any of your officers in danger. We didn't anticipate this kind of response from the man and woman we're pursuing."

"You anticipated wrong."

"Yes, sir. And I'm pissed off, too, believe me."

Burns kept his cool. The chief had every right to lay into him. He would be doing the same thing if the shoe were on the opposite foot. Plus, he really needed the chief's help right now. So he was eager to make peace. Without a fight to be had, Jackson let loose one more angry huff, unclenched his fists, and gathered himself.

"Well, there's no use wasting time standing here and arguing about the details. Doesn't bring Tommy back. I just want this guy captured and brought to justice."

"Same," Burns agreed.

"What do you need from us?"

"Were there any witnesses to the shooting?"

"None yet. But it's still early."

"What about body cam footage?"

"The kid unfortunately didn't have it turned on. It all happened so fast."

"What's the latest on the hunt for our fugitive?"

"My guys are searching, but there's been no sign of him. It's a madhouse over there. Hard to tell one thing from another; people have been rushing off all over. He could be damn near anywhere at this point."

"Right." Burns's mind was bouncing in all directions. "How many ways in and out of town?"

Jackson twisted up his mouth. "Probably a half dozen or so, if you include isolated back roads. But it's mainly Highway 40 in both directions. Berthoud Pass, that way." He pointed over Burns's shoulder, then stuck a thumb over his own shoulder the opposite way. "And through Granby and Hot Sulphur Springs that way."

"Can you shut down Berthoud Pass?"

"I can do whatever the hell I want. I'm the chief of police."

"Good. We need to do whatever we possibly can to confine them to this immediate area. If they somehow get out, we could be screwed. These people have proven to be very elusive. If you can manage it, let's do everything we can to create checkpoints at all exits out of town. I don't care if you use firemen, medics, or even local ranchers—whatever it takes. We just need armed men with flashlights and phones."

Jackson spun his weight around and snapped his fingers at an officer lingering behind him, who quickly hustled over. "Close the pass

ASAP. And call Chief Logan over in Granby. Tell him we need a block-ade on 40 immediately and all the help we can get over here. We also need checkpoints on all roads out of the valley. Use whoever the hell you can find. Just get them all blocked. And make sure everyone has the suspect's photo."

The officer rushed off with his orders.

"Best I can do," Jackson said, turning back to Burns.

"Do you know all the police chiefs within, say, a sixty-mile radius?"

"Been on the job nearly forty years. I know everyone."

"Can you call them all and get them up to speed? Let's see how many reinforcements we can get over here as quickly as possible."

"What about the media?"

"What about them?"

"I know all the TV guys, too. They could help us get the word out."

Burns had been afraid he'd bring that up. Every small-town police chief he'd ever met relished a chance to stand in front of TV cameras. "Let's hold off on that for now. We don't need every drunk cowboy from Denver to Grand Junction calling in and claiming they spotted them. These first couple of hours are critical. In my experience, that would only make our jobs more difficult."

"All right. Let me know if you change your mind. I'm good in front of the cameras."

"Will do."

Jackson sighed, shifted his girth. "I gotta drive over to my nephew's house now and tell his pretty wife what just happened to him. Just the thought of it makes me nauseous. You ever have to do something like this, Burns?"

"Yes, unfortunately. It's the worst part of the job."

"Yeah. Promise me we'll catch the bastard who did this to Tommy."

"With your help, Chief, we have a much better chance."

FOURTEEN

Cole drove precisely the speed limit down Highway 40 through the small towns of Fraser and Tabernash on the way to Granby, even though everything inside him wanted to stomp on the gas pedal. But the last thing he could afford right now was to have a cop pull him over for stupidly speeding. He glanced over at Lisa, who was hunched in the passenger seat as to not be seen from the road. Jade was lying down in the back seat, as instructed. They rode in near silence. Mainly because he and Lisa didn't want to talk about too much in front of Jade. Cole certainly wasn't going to share what had happened to him back in town yet. The circumstances they were facing were already terrifying enough, and he was freaking out on the inside. He wanted more time to process what had happened before rolling that bomb out there.

Cole watched every passing car closely. It was late. The highway was not busy. This made him feel exposed. He wondered if the police were already searching for Lisa's car. If not, he knew it would be happening shortly. Both of their vehicles were officially registered with the state. They needed to dump the Subaru ASAP.

Cole suddenly cursed, stiffened in his seat. He could see police vehicles with red and blue blinking lights coming straight toward him on Highway 40.

"What is it?" Lisa asked. She couldn't see above the dashboard.

"Police. Up ahead, coming this way. Probably from Grandy."

"Do you need to get off the main road?"

"There's no other way to get to the unit."

"Do you think they're coming for us?"

Cole swallowed. "We're about to find out."

He tucked his head low, held his breath, as three police vehicles sped past him. His eyes locked on his rearview mirror. Lisa couldn't help herself—she rose and turned in her seat to also look back down the highway.

"They're not turning around," she said, exhaling.

"Why are the police even after us?" Jade asked from the back.

"It's just . . . a misunderstanding," Cole replied weakly.

"A misunderstanding?" Jade retorted. "Dad, I'm not stupid! You don't have multiple police cars show up at your house because of a misunderstanding."

"You're right, honey," Lisa said. "It's complicated."

"Did you break the law, Dad? Did you steal money or something?"

"If I've broken any laws, it's only to protect my family."

"What does that even mean?" Jade replied. "So . . . you did break the law?"

"Get down!" Cole said, as two more police cars were suddenly in view around a twist in the highway.

Both Lisa and Jade dropped back into their hidden positions. Cole also felt the urge to scoot down in his seat this time, his nerves nearly shot, as both police vehicles again raced past them without incident.

"We're good?" Lisa asked.

He nodded. "Hopefully all these police cars racing toward Winter Park means the FBI believes we're still camped out there somewhere. We need the head start."

"The FBI!" Jade exclaimed, her voice cracking. "Are you serious, Dad?"

Cole sighed, annoyed with himself for letting that slip out. "Yes."

"Wait . . . doesn't the FBI mainly go after terrorists? Is that what you are? A terrorist?"

"No," he said, but didn't elaborate. He turned onto a dirt road inside the Granby city limits. They were almost there. He was breathing a little easier.

"You guys can't do this to me," Jade continued, getting herself worked up. "This is not fair. You have to tell me what's going on. It's my birthday, Dad! I'm not a little kid anymore. Whatever it is, I can handle it. Just tell me."

Cole hit the brakes, the car skidding to a stop on the gravel road.

He turned around to face Jade. "Baby, do you trust me?"

She hesitantly nodded.

"Do you trust your mom?" he said.

"Yes."

"Do you believe we love you, and we'd do everything in our power to protect you?"

"Of course. It's just—"

"Then no more questions for now, Jade. When we get somewhere we can stop and breathe for a moment, we will tell you everything. I promise. But this back-and-forth with you right now isn't helping us. Okay?"

He could tell she didn't like that, but she nodded just the same. He floored the gas again, the tires spinning. A half mile down the road, he pulled up to a property with a secured gate and a big red sign that said GILLEY'S AUTO AND BOAT STORAGE. There was a rusted keypad in the short driveway. Cole rolled down his window, tried to type in a code he'd used dozens of times before. The digital box above the keypad flashed ERROR: Code 14. He typed the code again. Same result. ERROR: Code 14.

Cole cursed. This was bad. He did it a third time without success.

"Is it the right code?" Lisa asked.

"Of course. You think I'd forget the code?"

"No, I just . . . what is going on?"

"The damn automatic gate isn't working."

"Cole, everything is in there," Lisa said, panic surging up in her voice. "How're we going to get the van? This is the only way in and out."

Cole pounded on the steering wheel, racking his brain. He'd never anticipated something like this happening. He'd never had any issues with the automatic gate. He knew if they left in the Subaru right now, they likely wouldn't get very far. That couldn't be their only option. He studied the gate for a moment. It wasn't a big, reinforced steel number. It was cheaper looking, with thin metal bars and some mesh wire. Could he blast through it?

"Both of you get out of the car," he instructed.

"Why?" Lisa asked.

"So I can get us inside the property."

Lisa and Jade climbed out of the vehicle and stood off to the side in the grass. Cole shifted the car into reverse, backed straight out into the dirt road, and then put the vehicle back into drive. He pushed the brake pedal fully down, revved the engine, and then released the brake. The surprisingly powerful Subaru rocketed forward toward the gate. Gripping the steering wheel tightly, Cole ducked his head at impact. The vehicle collided violently with the gate, ripping it from its hinges and deploying the car's airbags in the process. Cole's head slammed forward against the airbag and then back against the headrest. He hit the brakes again, bringing the car to a stop, and pushed the already deflating airbag away from his view. His face felt like he'd just been punched by a prizefighter. But it had worked. The gate lay flat on the asphalt. He could see the front end of their Subaru crumpled up and slightly smoking. Something had flown up and put a huge crack in the windshield. The car suddenly went dead on him. He tried to start it back up but got no response from the vehicle.

Opening the car door, Cole stumbled out.

Lisa and Jade rushed up to him.

"Are you okay?" Lisa said.

He was dazed but okay. "Yes, I'm good. But the car won't start. We'll have to go on foot from here."

After grabbing their bags, Cole took off running, Lisa and Jade on his heels, and followed the main storage facility drive all the way to the back. The place was full of covered slips. Boats on trailers—some of which looked like they'd been sitting there for twenty years—as well as company cargo trucks and several rows of RVs. Their parking slip was just around the corner and to the left. Cole was thankful there were no other people currently on the property. In that regard, the automatic gate system being down had aided them tonight. The last thing he needed was to run into someone trying to pick up or drop off their boat. He wanted to get in and out without being seen.

Cole hustled up to an old white van with faded blue lettering on both sides that said GUNDERSON FAMILY PLUMBERS. He'd purchased the van a few weeks after they'd moved to Winter Park ten years ago. The company had gone out of business. He visited the storage unit once a month to take the van out for a quick drive to make sure everything was running okay. He'd probably put only three hundred miles on it in ten years. Lisa came to the unit twice a year to switch out the clothes stuffed in three large duffel bags in the back—mainly to keep up with Jade's rapid growth—as well as update a small collection of nonperishable food items in a plastic cooler. The last two times she'd insisted Cole come here alone with the updated clothes and food. She said she didn't even want to be on the property anymore, it was so depressing.

Cole found the key sitting on top of the back right tire and unlocked the vehicle.

"What are we doing here?" Jade said. "If I'm even allowed to ask that."

"Switching vehicles," Cole said.

His daughter's face scrunched up. "For this old thing?"

"Yes," he said.

"Does it even run?"

"Like a charm," he said. "At least it did a month ago, when I was last here."

Cole climbed into the driver's seat, stuck the key in the ignition, and the vehicle started right up. "Hallelujah," he whispered. Lisa was already busy tossing Jade's backpack into the back of the van. She returned with a small gray bag, set it on the ground, unzipped it, and pulled out a black leather hair kit. She looked over at Cole, who was checking things out on the van's dashboard.

"You still want to do this?" she asked, holding up the bag.

He turned. "Yes, for sure."

He quickly got out, sat on the dirt ground right in front of Lisa, while Jade curiously watched what was going on. Lisa unzipped the bag and pulled out a pair of hair scissors. While Jade gasped, Lisa began chopping off big locks of his wavy hair, working quickly, getting it all as close to the scalp as possible. Then she switched to a battery-powered hair trimmer and began going to town, until his head was completely shaved. A pile of hair sat on his shoulders and on the ground around him. When she was finished, Cole took the hair trimmer from her and started working on his beard, using the shortest trimming option available to him. Within minutes, nearly all his head and facial hair had completely vanished. It felt strange, considering he'd had the longer hair and the beard for the entire time they'd lived in Colorado.

"I don't even recognize you," Lisa said, shaking her head.

"That's the point, right?"

"I guess. It just . . . sucks."

"Yeah, I know. But it'll grow back."

"Dad, you look so weird," Jade said.

He held up the trimmer. "You're next."

Her eyes went wide. "No!"

He forced a smile. "Just kidding."

"That's not funny."

But she smiled back at him, which was nice to see. They could all use a little levity right now. It was important for them to survive this both emotionally and physically.

Lisa pulled two black baseball caps out of the bag. One was branded with the University of Colorado, the other the Denver Broncos.

"Which one do you want?" she asked Jade.

"I have to wear a cap?"

"Yes, and stuff all your hair inside. Unless you want to go Dad's route."

"No, thanks. I'll take the CU one."

Lisa handed it over, placed the Broncos cap on her own head, and began shoving as much of her hair as possible up underneath. Jade did the same.

"I need to patch up your arm," Lisa said to Cole. "That's a pretty gnarly gash."

She pulled a first aid kit out of the bag, cleaned the wound with antiseptic wipes, wrapped his arm with gauze, and then sealed it with white medical tape to stop it from bleeding any further. Then she asked Jade to put the bag into the back of the van.

Lisa leaned into his ear, whispered, "You going to tell me what really happened?"

"Yes," he whispered back. "Later."

She huffed. "Fine."

Cole slid open the back door to the van's cargo area. "Okay, both of you climb in the back. We need to get moving."

Jade walked over, poked her head inside. "Wait, there are no seats back here."

"We'll be fine," Lisa said. "We have two beanbags. Come on."

She climbed inside, followed by Jade. Two fluffy pink beanbags had been inside the vehicle for nearly a decade. Lisa dropped into one of them.

"This is crazy," Jade objected. "What about seatbelts?"

"Your dad is an excellent driver," Lisa said. "Sit down."

Jade hesitantly sat in the second beanbag. Cole moved into the driver's seat. He took a quick peek at himself in the rearview mirror. What he saw staring back was almost shocking. The last time he'd seen this guy was back in high school, when the whole soccer team had decided to shave their heads during the playoffs. But he looked nothing like the man the FBI and the police had just tried to chase down in the park.

He started the van again, put it into drive, began to pull out.

"Can I at least ask where we are going?" Jade said.

Cole adjusted his rearview mirror to see his daughter. "You like the beach, don't you?"

"Yes, but we've only been like twice. And it's been forever."

"Then I guess we're due a beach trip."

Jade glanced over at her mom. "Are we seriously going to the beach right now?"

"If we can get away from here." Lisa sighed.

"Where? What beach?"

Cole said, "A beautiful little town on the Pacific coast called Sayulita."

"Is that in California?"

"No, we're going to Mexico."

FIFTEEN

Brock Gunner pulled a gray Ford Bronco onto a neighborhood street and parked with a distant view of Cole and Lisa Shipley's house around the corner. There were cops and FBI agents damn near everywhere. Just like there were cops and FBI agents everywhere at the city park he'd just left. It was chaos back there, which had at least made it easy for him to get out without any extra trouble. Brock couldn't stop cursing himself. He'd been a split second away from taking care of his first and probably most important target, and he didn't squeeze the damn trigger in time. He'd failed. He'd completely underestimated Cole Shipley. The man's swift and surprisingly powerful kick had come out of nowhere. In hindsight, he should've shot Shipley first before putting a second bullet into the cop. He kept replaying this tactical error in his head and getting more pissed off. Plus, he didn't like killing cops. Brock would've had no problem taking out an FBI agent. The Feds were liars and bullies, and the family had endured several unfair government battles over the years. But cops were different. Brock had several friends back in Texas who were police officers, including one of his own cousins.

Brock picked up his cell phone, texted: Things didn't go as planned.

Again, an immediate response: I heard. What the hell happened? You kill that cop?

Had no choice. He was about to arrest Shipley.

Then how the hell did Shipley get away from you?

Brock didn't feel like explaining it. It made him look weak.
He texted: He got lucky.

That's the second time he's gotten lucky with you.

Brock didn't respond. It was the brutal truth.
The man texted again: You have no clue where Shipley went?

No. But I'm parked down the street from his house right now.

Don't bother. None of our targets are there.

All of them are gone?

Yes. Police are setting up roadblocks, trying to trap
them in the valley.

What do you want me to do?

Stay close. Be ready. You take your rifle?

Yes.

Brock owned a Fierce Rogue backcountry hunting rifle, one of
the best on the market. It was incredibly lightweight and amazingly
accurate, especially in his hands. He'd taken a beer can off the top of a
fence post from more than a thousand yards out when competing with
some buddies. The rifle was in the bag sitting in the Bronco's back seat.

Good. You may have to do this from a distance.

Distance is not a problem.

Yes, I know. Shipley say anything to the cop?

Didn't get a chance. I stopped it.

Good. Don't let this get away from us.

I won't fail again.

SIXTEEN

Cole drove hesitantly back toward Winter Park. The fastest way south through Colorado, New Mexico, and eventually on to El Paso, where he planned to cross the US and Mexico border, was Interstate 25. Which meant driving the Berthoud Pass out of the valley and crossing over toward Denver. Any other way out of the valley could take several more hours. The map app on his burner phone told him it was eleven hours to El Paso. And then another eighteen hours from there to their final destination: Sayulita, a village on Mexico's Pacific coast backed by the Sierra Madre Occidental mountains. Population was around three thousand, plus a steady flow of tourists. Cole and Lisa had vacationed there when they were newlyweds. Sayulita had picturesque beaches, charming restaurants, and a relaxed atmosphere—unlike the hustle and bustle of the more prominent tourist resorts. They'd vowed to go back someday. He just never expected it to be under these conditions. But he felt the tiny beach town would be a great place to get lost for a while and start over.

He didn't expect getting across the border to be an issue for them. He'd recently had a new set of fake passports created by a foreign contact, with whom he had remained connected under an alias. Cole had created and ditched so many aliases over the years he could hardly keep up with all of them. At this very moment, he had three different sets of fake identities in his bag. They could become the Jensens, the Fosters, or the Rutters. He would sort that out later with Lisa and Jade, who would undoubtedly be stunned.

First, they had to get out of the valley. He felt his heart begin to race as he reentered Winter Park's city limits. There was a lot of traffic as he drove slowly up Main Street because of the crowded scene around Hideaway Park, and traffic came to a crawl as everyone slowed to get a look at things. There were police vehicles parked up and down the street with red and blue lights blinking and officers nearly everywhere. Most seemed to be interviewing various groups of people.

"What's going on?" Lisa asked from the back of the van.

They'd been very quiet on the drive over from Granby.

"Driving through town."

"Why so slow?"

"There's still a mob of people and cars here."

"Are you sure this is the best way out?" Lisa asked.

"No, but it's definitely the fastest."

"Just don't let anyone recognize you."

"Believe me, I'm trying my best."

Both Lisa and Jade were still sitting on their beanbags in the back of the van and tucked out of view. Jade hadn't said much since he'd broken the news that they were leaving the country and headed to Mexico. Her mouth had dropped open, and her eyes went wide—and her face had basically stayed frozen like that for the past fifteen minutes. He knew this was a lot for his daughter to process. He'd had years to think about this moment and emotionally prepare himself. She'd had only a few minutes.

Cole felt his throat tighten up as he passed the park. He could see a collection of guys wearing matching dark-blue FBI jackets—the same jacket he'd seen in the back seat of the Ford Taurus earlier. He slouched down slightly behind the wheel. Even though he knew he looked dramatically different than he had earlier, it was not easy to be driving within fifty feet of several FBI agents whose only mission right now was to find and arrest them. He wondered who was leading the operation. Thirteen years ago it had been a special agent named Mark Burns. Cole had closely followed the investigation online, reading every single article he could find to try to stay one step ahead. He'd also researched everything he could find out about Burns—just in case they were ever put into the same room together and he needed to be able to appeal to the agent's own humanity. From what he remembered, Burns was married at that time and had a two-year-old daughter. She would now be one year older than Jade.

The FBI's pursuit of them had stayed active for several years, and then everything had just died off one day. Cole could no longer find articles and reports online anywhere. He'd presumed their case had been moved to a less urgent category. That's when he and Lisa had decided to relocate to Colorado and start over in the mountains. He'd thought about Agent Burns here and there over the years, and every once in a while would search him up. Last he'd checked, Burns was working out of the FBI's Washington, DC, office.

Cole kept the van inching forward. Big crowds were huddled everywhere watching the actions of the FBI agents and the police. He wondered what these people knew, if anything. Had it become public yet that he and Lisa were fugitives? Did everyone in town now have his photo on their phones? Cole thought about the private school where he'd taught history for the past eight years. The staff were going to be shocked. But he mostly mourned for his students. He'd given so much to cultivate deep and lasting relationships with the kids at the school all these years. Those efforts would now be obliterated in a single moment when the news finally broke about Mr. Shipley. The kids would undoubtedly feel betrayed.

Cole sighed. That was too painful to think about right now.

He kept the van creeping down Main Street and slowly passed by the opening of the alley where he'd barely escaped gunfire earlier. He saw an ambulance and two police vehicles parked at the curb and groaned when he spotted two uniformed medics wheeling a cart out of the alley with what looked like a black body bag on it. He presumed the dead police officer was inside.

"What is it?" Lisa asked from the back.

"Nothing. Stay down."

Cole had still not mentioned anything about what happened in the alley. He wanted to delay that conversation, as to not add any more fuel to the bonfire of fear they were already dealing with right now. But he knew he would have to explain everything to Lisa soon.

Traffic began to finally pick up speed as they cleared midtown and began heading east on 40 toward the Berthoud Pass. Cole pushed down on the gas pedal, got the van rolling, and began breathing easier. Thankfully, the van was running great. It had passed inspection at an auto shop three months ago. He just hoped there were no high-speed chases in their future. He wasn't sure the vehicle would even accelerate past seventy miles per hour. He checked his watch. It should take them about thirty minutes to get up and down the pass. There was nothing but highways on the other side of the mountain. They should be home free.

He finally heard Jade speak again and tell her mom she was hungry. Lisa grabbed the small cooler, opened it, and began rummaging through various granola bars, chips, cookies, and other assorted snack items.

"You want anything?" Lisa asked Cole.

"Shot of bourbon," he said, flashing a small smile at her in the rearview mirror.

Again, he was trying whatever he could to lighten the intensity of the moment.

She gave him the slightest of grins back. "No bourbon. But I do have wine. And I may just pop it open and drink straight from the bottle."

"Save some for me."

Cole's smile suddenly disappeared. He cursed under his breath.

"What, Dad?" Jade asked.

He slowed the van behind a row of other vehicles, who were all coming to a sudden stop. He tried to peer around them up ahead. He cursed again—there was a police vehicle parked horizontally across the road, and it looked like the gate to the pass was closed behind it. A police officer stood in the road, using a hand to instruct everyone to turn around, one at a time, while he also shined a flashlight into the front of each car.

"We're in trouble," Cole said. "They closed the pass."

SEVENTEEN

Sixty-seven minutes. That's how long Burns and his FBI team had been on the ground in Winter Park, and yet they still had little to show for it. And it certainly wasn't from a lack of local support. The police presence had grown exponentially with help from several other regional departments, so there were twice as many officers out patrolling the streets. All exits from the area had been manned by police for the past fifteen minutes. Everyone with a badge was now on the lookout for a green Subaru Outback registered to Cole and Lisa Shipley. But there had been no reported sightings. Their whereabouts remained unknown. And Burns was beyond frustrated. He kept asking himself the same questions: Where the hell could they have gone? Had they stayed prepared all these years to make a quick exit? Was that how they'd disappeared so quickly and easily? Were they already out of the valley? Had he made a massive mistake delaying a potential arrest until he arrived?

Burns and Davis had just finished interviewing all the neighbors on the Shipleys' street, asking who had seen or knew what, but they all seemed mostly clueless, and shocked. *Cole and Lisa? No way. They knew them so well. This couldn't be right. They'd been neighbors for eight years. There had been nothing odd or mysterious about the family. They were always kind, helpful, and fun to be around.* And so on and so forth. But Burns's final interview had produced a kernel of hope. One of the teenage boys on the street mentioned Jade Shipley had a boyfriend named Tyler Healey, who lived over in Tabernash. The neighbor boy was good friends with Tyler—they mountain biked together all the time. He said Jade and Tyler had been texting a lot lately and had started hanging out. Burns was leery of the claim, since he'd found no evidence of such a relationship in Jade's bedroom. But maybe she'd been hiding it from her father. Izzy hid damn near everything about boys from him.

Burns and Davis drove over to Tabernash in one of the black Tahoes and pulled up to a log cabin–style house that had probably been built thirty years earlier. A Toyota Highlander was parked out front next to a Nissan Rogue. They both got out and approached the front door. It was after eleven, so most of the lights were off inside, but Burns had no time to be respectful of people's sleep right now. Every second mattered. He knocked on the front door and waited. Davis was busy working his cell phone, searching social media for Tyler Healey.

"The kid has two accounts I can find so far," Davis mentioned. "And there are several recent photos of him with Jade Shipley. They are clearly more than friends. Lots of hand-holding and hugging."

"We've still found no social media belonging to Jade?"

Davis shook his head. "Nothing. Just like with her parents."

"Not a surprise."

There was no immediate answer at the door, so Burns banged even louder. This time a light popped on down the hallway. A moment later the door opened, showing a fortysomething man with curly brown hair wearing sweatpants and a white T-shirt. He looked half-asleep and kept blinking, like he was trying to get his eyes to work correctly.

"Are you Robert Healey?" Burns asked.

"Yes. What's, uh . . . what's going on?"

Burns and Davis flashed their FBI credentials in near unison, like they'd been doing regularly for the past hour.

"I'm Special Agent Burns with the FBI. This is Agent Davis. Sorry to wake you. But we need to speak with your son, Mr. Healey. It's urgent."

The mention of the FBI seemed to jolt Healey awake. "Wait . . . what? Is my son in some kind of trouble?"

"No, sir. We just have some questions for him regarding his relationship with a girl named Jade Shipley."

"Jade? Has something happened to her?"

"Let's wait to talk about it with your son."

"Yeah, okay, please come on in. Let me go get him. He's upstairs."

Healey led Burns and Davis into a small, outdated living room and turned on the lights. Then he went upstairs while they both stood there and waited. Seconds later, the man returned with an athletic-looking teenage boy with bushy hair wearing boxers and a Colorado Rockies T-shirt. The boy didn't look like he'd been sleeping, which was no surprise. From Burns's experience, teenagers stayed up nearly all night on the weekends. When Izzy was with him, he'd sometimes find her still on her phone after three in the morning when he got up to go to the bathroom. Then she'd want to sleep all day and act annoyed if he tried to wake her.

"Son, these are FBI agents," Healey said. "They have some questions."

"I'm Agent Burns, this is Agent Davis."

Tyler's eyes went wide. He nodded but said nothing. Burns wanted to put him at ease. He didn't need the kid clamming up on him when they desperately needed information.

"You like the Rockies?" he asked the boy, pointing at his shirt.

Another quick nod.

"I don't," said Burns, smiling. "Not after your boys swept my Nationals last week. We couldn't touch your pitching staff. Especially Carlson. He's red-hot right now."

The boy gave a slight grin. "Yeah, we're four games up on the Dodgers."

"Might just be your year."

"I hope so. My dad said we'll get tickets if they make the playoffs."

The tactic seemed to work. The kid was loosening up.

"Cool. Can you sit down with us for a second?"

"Yeah, all right, I guess."

They all found spots on uncomfortable furniture around the living room. The father offered them something to drink, which they both declined.

"How long have you known Jade?" Burns began.

Tyler swallowed. "Is she okay? Has something happened?"

Burns and Davis glanced at each other.

"Why're you asking us that, Tyler?" Davis said.

"She hasn't been responding to any of my texts tonight. And now two FBI agents are sitting five feet away from me asking questions about her. So, yeah, seems pretty obvious."

"Be respectful, Tyler," the father said.

"Sorry," the boy quickly apologized.

Burns leaned forward. "We're looking for Jade and her parents right now."

Tyler's eyes narrowed. "They're not at home?"

"No. And we were hoping you might know where we can find them."

Tyler studied them a moment. "Why're you looking for them?"

Burns didn't want to divulge the truth just yet. It might cloud the conversation. So he tried a different route. "For their own protection. Especially for Jade."

This didn't seem to satisfy him. "Protection from who? What's going on?"

Davis spoke up. "We're not at liberty to say, Tyler. It's a highly classified matter. But we can tell you that Jade is in real danger. We have to find her. Which is why we're here. When was the last time you heard from her?"

This seemed to compel the boy in a positive way. He looked at his phone and used a finger to scroll. "Nine twenty-eight tonight. She texted me to tell me how much she liked my birthday present and enjoyed hanging out with me today. It's her birthday, you know?"

"Yes, we do," Burns said. "Was there any communication after that?"

Tyler shook his head. "I keep texting her, but she isn't responding."

"Is that unusual?" Davis questioned.

"Yeah, for sure. We usually text each other until one of us falls asleep. It's been that way for the last two weeks straight. But not tonight. I knew something was wrong."

"Do you mind if we take a look at your texts from tonight?" Burns asked.

"You want my phone?" Tyler said, clutching his phone tightly, as if they were asking him to donate a vital organ. Izzy acted the same way with her phone. Like handing it over for even a few seconds might cut off her oxygen.

"Yes," Burns said. "We'll give it right back."

Tyler looked over at his dad for either rescue or reassurance, who told him to do it. So the kid hesitantly handed the phone over to Burns. Both he and Davis did a quick review. As the boy had mentioned, Jade had texted Tyler around nine thirty to thank him for the present. Then there were a half dozen follow-up texts from Tyler over the past hour and a half asking what she was doing and why she wasn't responding. The timing made sense considering the police had arrived at the Shipleys' house only ten minutes after her last text—finding them gone. The tone of her text to Tyler made Burns believe Jade did not know she was about to flee with her family. He did a quick scroll up and scanned other messages between them from the past couple of days. There were literally hundreds. Mostly emojis and abbreviated slang he would never understand. There was nothing that seemed relevant to the current situation. Just awkward teenage love banter. He'd read the same exact thing on Izzy's phone while she was sleeping at his condo. Of course, his daughter didn't know he had access. She'd probably never talk to him again if she did. But he couldn't help himself. He wanted to know (and investigate) what boys she liked. So far, none of them had a juvenile record, at least.

He set the phone on the coffee table. "Was Jade acting unusual today?"

Tyler shook his head. "No, sir. She was really happy."

"Was there any mention of her family going somewhere tonight?"

"Like where?"

"Out of town."

"No, Jade would've told me. We're supposed to hang out tomorrow."

Davis said, "Has she ever mentioned anything to you about her parents having a second place somewhere? Like a condo? Or a cabin? A rental property? Anything like that?"

Tyler frowned. "No, sir. Her dad is only a schoolteacher. And her mom barely even works part-time. I don't think they have much money. Jade actually told me they hadn't gone on a real vacation in years because money was so tight. That's also why she hasn't been able to get the surgery she needs. It's way too expensive."

"What kind of surgery?" Burns asked.

"Spinal fusion surgery. She has severe scoliosis. This past year, she started dealing with a lot of pain and even had to stop cheering. But her dad told her today they were finally going to be able to do the surgery. She was so happy about it."

Burns thought about the offshore account Cole had accessed this morning. It now made sense why he'd risked transferring the money out after letting it sit dormant for all these years. He was doing it for his daughter. That sat heavy with him for a second. He would've done the same thing for Izzy. But it would cost Cole his freedom.

"How well do you know her parents?" Burns asked.

The boy shrugged. "Her mom is pretty cool. We've spoken a couple of times. I haven't met her dad yet. Jade keeps saying he'd freak out if he even knew we were hanging out."

Burns grinned. "Girls' dads can be like that sometimes." He leaned forward, changed directions. "Jade ever tell you anything about her parents' past?"

"What do you mean?" Tyler said.

"Like when they were younger. Or places they've lived before."

"Not really. They used to live in Denver. That's where Jade was born. I think her mom grew up somewhere in Arizona. Jade has pictures of her mom back when she was a high school cheerleader."

Burns nodded. The first part was of course a lie—Jade had obviously not been born in Denver. But the second part, about Lisa Shipley once being a high school cheerleader in Arizona, was true. He'd been wondering all evening if Jade knew anything at all about their family's real origin story. Had they kept everything about their past a secret from her?

"Is texting the way you two communicate?" he asked the boy.

"Yes, sir. I mean, we also talk on the phone sometimes. But we mainly text."

Burns knew he could confiscate the boy's phone as evidence, if he wanted. But he had other plans and needed to keep it in Tyler's possession. Out of questions, he stood, thanked Tyler and his dad for their time, and then pulled two business cards from his wallet and handed them out. "If you hear from her, will you please call me and let me know? We want to keep her safe, Tyler. But we can only do that if we find her and her parents."

The boy nodded and seemed relieved the conversation was over.

A moment later, Burns and Davis were back inside the Tahoe and debriefing.

"You think he knows more than he's saying?" Davis asked.

"Doubtful. The kid was too scared to lie to us."

"Yeah," Davis agreed. "So what do you want to do?"

"I think there will be more communication at some point, if up to Jade. Young love does not easily fade, Agent Davis. I've eavesdropped plenty of times on Izzy when she's talking to one of her boyfriends. When she's in that place of teenage euphoria, she can't go more than a couple of hours without texting or calling him."

"You think Tyler will contact us when she does?"

"Not a chance. Let's monitor his phone."

"I'll make it happen ASAP."

EIGHTEEN

They were stopped in the car line at the blocked pass.

Lisa anxiously scooted up toward him. "Are they searching vehicles?"

Cole watched closely. "Yes, sort of. Just quick looks with a flashlight."

"Can you turn around before getting up there?" Lisa asked.

He shook his head. "Not without drawing attention to us."

"Maybe Jade and I should climb out the back. You could pick us up on your return."

He glanced in his rearview mirror. "How're we going to explain that to the row of cars building up behind us? It would be like shining a huge spotlight on ourselves."

"So what do we do?"

"Get under the blankets. Don't move. Don't make a sound. I'll handle it."

Lisa squeezed his arm, then moved into the back again. Cole felt his heart racing as he drew even closer to the police officer. They were five cars back. He racked his brain for any alternative to having a flashlight beam hit his face but couldn't come up with anything. The officer turned a Jeep Wrangler around. Four cars now. In the back, Lisa grabbed two thick blankets they'd stored in the van. She handed one to

Jade. Cole watched his daughter's face in the rearview mirror and could see it growing paler by the second.

"Everything will be okay," he said, trying to reassure her.

"Right," Jade muttered. "This is completely insane."

But she did what she was told. Both now had blankets over them. The cargo area of the van was dark. They were three cars back. Cole kept reminding himself to breathe as normally as possible. He couldn't look uneasy right now. He had to find his poker face. He wondered if the officer would want to examine the back of the van. To this point, there had been only cars and trucks turning around in front of him. The officer had not searched the trunks of any cars, but a van might be a different story. Two cars back. He watched as the officer shined his flashlight inside a Jeep Cherokee. Just a pop of light at the male driver in the front. The officer then did a quick glance at his cell phone. He said something to the driver, who quickly turned his vehicle around in the street and headed back toward Winter Park. The officer clearly had photos of them on his phone. Cole was about to find out if his dramatic makeover would work. He hadn't expected to test it so soon.

The small car in front of him got a quick scan. It looked like a lady with curly hair was driving. The officer smiled at her and waved her around into a U-turn in the road. They were next. He eased the van forward. It was go time.

"Not a peep," he whispered to the back.

The officer stepped up toward the driver side of the van. He looked to be about Cole's age, with slightly graying hair. Cole felt his heart pumping so fast he wondered if the officer would be able to notice it from the outside. He took one last deep breath, let it out slowly, then smiled wide as he rolled down the van's window. He felt the flashlight beam hit him square in the face, blinding him for a moment.

"Evening, officer. We got an accident or something?"

"No, sir. Just a police emergency. Pass is closed."

The flashlight remained on him for a few very uncomfortable seconds. It felt like forever. Was the officer putting it together? Was he a dead man? If the officer asked him to get out of the van, Cole knew he'd have no choice but to aggressively react. His plan was to punch the gas while doing a swift U-turn, hoping the officer would feel compelled to protect himself and get out of the way. Cole would then speed back down the street and out of view, pull off somewhere short of town near the ski resort, and immediately ditch the van. From there, he wasn't sure. They might be forced to run deep into the woods of the mountains and hide out for the night until he could figure out their next move.

He hated the plan and quickly prayed he wouldn't have to utilize it.

The flashlight finally left his face, hit the passenger seat.

"Who you looking for?" Cole asked, as casually as possible.

"Couple of dangerous individuals."

"Really? Here in the valley? That's crazy."

"You don't even know the half of it. I need to peek in the back, if you don't mind."

Cole felt fear grip him. He set his foot lightly on the gas pedal and squeezed the steering wheel in his right hand. Thinking fast, he said, "Sure. But just to warn you, it's disgusting back there. Had to deal with the worst sewer backup situation I've ever seen this evening. Spent three hours up to my ankles in poop water. Worst part of the job."

The officer flashed his light on the side of the van. "You work for Teddy Gunderson?"

The van had previously belonged to Gunderson Family Plumbers. He went with it. It was a last desperate effort to keep their feet beneath them. "Yep."

"I thought he closed up shop years ago."

"He did. But we're up and running again."

The officer nodded, pressed his lips together. "Well, tell the old man I said hello. He and my pop used to go hunting together back when I was a kid. Teddy's a good man."

"He is a good man. I will definitely tell him."

"All right, you have a good night now."

The officer stepped back, casually waved Cole to turn around. It seemed the small connecting point was enough to keep him from getting the back of the van searched. Cole quickly turned the vehicle around in the street, eased forward back toward town. He didn't take another breath until he was a hundred yards down the road.

"You can come out now," he said, exhaling.

He watched in his rearview mirror as both Lisa and Jade pulled the blankets off them.

"That was way too close," Lisa said, matching his shortness of breath.

"Wow, Dad," Jade interjected, a touch of excitement in her voice. "You were *so cool* under pressure back there."

"Well, it wasn't my first time."

Jade tilted her head. "What do you mean?"

"We were just fortunate."

"So where to now?" Lisa asked, her voice rising. "We're going to have to get off 40. I presume they'll have the other way blocked by now as well. And maybe even the side roads. There are not a lot of routes out of this area, Cole. We could be stuck in this valley."

"We have to find a way."

"Any ideas?"

"Not yet. Let me know if you spot a helicopter somewhere."

This time she didn't offer him a smile. He couldn't blame her. This was a dire situation. They drove all the way back through Winter Park, again slowing in traffic around the park, before eventually reaching the other side of town. Cole then passed through Fraser and got out onto the open highway again. He passed by a couple of isolated county roads he knew would get them through the mountains and out safely on the other side. But as expected, both were now blocked by police officers. They crossed all the way through the town of Granby, and then he noticed traffic beginning to slow up ahead. A major roadblock on Highway 40. Two police vehicles. Instead of getting in line again, Cole quickly turned into a gas station parking lot. He stopped the van at the edge and tried to give himself space to think.

"This is bad, Cole," Lisa said, up next to him again.

There was so much desperation in her voice.

"I know," he agreed. "I didn't expect them to be able to block the roads so fast."

"Maybe we should hide out somewhere overnight. Hope they clear the roads in the morning. Try to make our way out then."

"We can't do that, Lisa. The police presence here in the valley will continue to grow. The longer we're here, the more likely we'll be found."

"Okay, then what?"

"I could try to talk my way through a roadblock again."

"No way. We got lucky the first time. We can't risk it twice."

"You're probably right. Dammit."

They both ducked down when another police vehicle with red and blue lights blinking sped past the gas station on Highway 40. Grand County Sheriff's Department. The police were even coming in from Hot Sulphur Springs. That made him think of his friend, Jacob, who worked Animal Control for the sheriff's department over there. He was a good guy. They'd fished together several times. An idea suddenly materialized in his head.

He quickly pulled back onto Highway 40 and drove the opposite direction.

"Where are you going?" Lisa asked.

"Fishing."

"What?"

"Give me a second, and I'll show you."

Five miles up the road, Cole again passed a stationary police vehicle blocking a county road intersection. A hefty cop was currently talking to someone in an old truck. About two hundred yards down from the intersection, Cole pulled off onto a gravel entrance in front of wide-open ranchland. He stopped in front of a cattle gate and quickly got out. He needed to be quick, as to not be spotted from the highway. The ranch belonged to the wealthy father of one of his former students. It had a huge, stocked fishing pond on the property. Because he was a favored teacher, Cole had been invited to use it whenever he wanted—which he did quite often. There was a combination lock on the cattle gate. Cole had stored the number code in his old cell phone, but he'd have to somehow pull it from memory now. He spun the lock back and forth. Pulled. It stayed locked. He tried another set of numbers. It remained locked. He tried a third time without success. And then a fourth. Dammit! He had so many numbers running through his cluttered brain right now.

He looked back over to the van, where both Lisa and Jade watched him closely through the windshield. He could see the hopelessness in Lisa's eyes. He had to remember this damn code already. It might be their only chance to escape from here. He studied the small lock, wondered if he could somehow break it off the gate with a rock or something. Not likely. He ran a hand over his shaved head, stared across the vast property. *Come on, Cole. Think hard.* Then another number set entered his mind, and he went back at it again. Bingo! He exhaled. After pulling open the gate, he got back into the van.

"Where are we?" Lisa asked him.

"The McNallys' ranch, where I fish all the time. They have about five hundred acres here. I just remembered there's a back entrance at the other end of the property. Cutting through the ranch will allow us to bypass the police roadblock."

"Really?"

He nodded. "We'll be able to get back on the county road on the other side."

"And where will that take us?"

"All the way over to Parshall. Thirty miles away."

"Thank God," she whispered. "Let's get out of here."

NINETEEN

Burns pulled into a storage property on the outskirts of Granby, eighteen miles down the road from Winter Park. A sign at the front said GILLEY'S AUTO AND BOAT STORAGE. Two police cars were parked just inside the entrance. An officer sat inside one of the SUVs, while another leaned against the other vehicle and talked on his phone. A skinny older man wearing denim overalls and a gray ski cap and smoking a cigarette also stood there with the police officer. Burns immediately noticed the security gate for the property had been knocked off its hinges and lay in a crumpled metal mess on the pavement. The owner of the storage facility had apparently stopped in around midnight, found the wreckage, and called the police. They'd discovered a battered green Subaru Outback with license plates matching their search.

"You think they kept an extra vehicle here?" Davis asked, sitting in the passenger seat.

"I doubt they came here to get their boat tonight."

"Right."

Burns eased the Tahoe through the entrance and stopped next to the wrecked Subaru. The front end of the vehicle was completely smashed up. It looked undrivable, which was probably why it had been abandoned at the front of the property. They both got out and circled the damaged Subaru. Burns opened the driver door. There wasn't much inside the vehicle. A package of wipes in the console, some loose change, couple of pens and hair bands—that was about it. Nothing at all in the back seat. He reached under the steering wheel and pulled the lever for the hatchback. The only thing they found in the back of the vehicle was a blue sports bag with a girl's T-shirt, shorts, socks, and athletic shoes.

They walked over to the officer standing beside his vehicle, made formalities.

Officer Marshall introduced the old man. "This is Jethro Gilley. He owns the facility."

"Can you tell me what happened?" Burns asked him, urgency in his tone.

"Not much to it. Stopped in 'bout twenty minutes ago. Found the damn front gate smashed to hell. Called the police. That's it."

"You have security cameras?" Davis asked him.

He bunched up his face, shook his head. "Nah, this ain't the dang Hyatt of storage properties, fellas. We're low-tech here. But I can keep the rent fair because of it."

Burns and Davis shared an annoyed glance. *Of course!*

Burns looked back at Jethro Gilley. "A guy named Cole Shipley rent here?"

Gilley pulled a folded piece of paper out of his pocket, unwrapped it. "Printed this out after I first got here. Wanted to see if I could tell if something had been stolen." He scanned the list. "Yeah, he's been renting a slip in the back."

"Take us to it."

"All right."

They followed Gilley through the property toward the back. Boats, RVs, and other vehicles were lined up back-to-back throughout, most protected under metal roofs.

Reaching the end, Gilley pointed toward an empty slip. "Right here."

If Cole Shipley had kept a vehicle here, it was now gone.

"For how long has he been a renter?" Burns asked Gilley.

"A longtimer. Ten years."

"So you know him?" Davis said.

"Nah. My boy mostly runs this place. He might. I only come here occasionally."

"Do you have any record of what he was storing here?" Burns asked.

Gilley shook his head again. "We don't pay no attention to that."

Burns blew out forcefully, frustrated. "Let me ask you something, Jethro. Why the hell would Cole Shipley smash through the front gate if he's a renter? Don't you give out codes or something?"

"Hell if I know," Gilley said, spitting on the ground. "Gonna cost me a dang fortune to have that gate replaced. Hope this Shipley guy has good insurance."

"Don't count on it," Davis mentioned.

Burns said, "I need you to get your son over here."

"Why?" Gilley asked.

"He might remember Shipley and know what was in this parking slip."

"Doubtful. He ain't the brightest."

"Still, call him. We need to talk to him ASAP."

"I done been trying to call him. He ain't answering. I talked to his girlfriend, though. She said he went over to Tin Cup earlier to play pool. Probably passed out drunk somewhere already. Boy is almost thirty, and I can't get him to grow up."

Burns turned to Officer Marshall. "We need to find him right away."

"Come with me, Mr. Gilley," said the officer. "Let's see what we can figure out."

Burns walked into the empty slip. There were no lights. When his forensic crew showed up in a few minutes, he would have them examine tire tracks and any other ground markings to see if they could sort out a particular type of vehicle. Had Lisa Shipley been here on her own with only her daughter? Or had they somehow rallied with Cole and all come over here together?

Either way, he didn't like it. One or all of them now had up to a two-hour head start in an unidentified vehicle. That was a major problem. However, someone still had to drive the vehicle. Hard to drive and hide at the same time. And the police had had every exit from the valley blocked by officers with high-resolution photos of the Shipleys for the past two hours. He could only hope that was enough to keep them confined to the local area.

Burns shined the flashlight on his phone around the parking slip. He noticed a pile of something on the dirt and bent down to take a better look. Then he cursed.

"That hair, boss?" Davis asked, joining him in the slip.

"Yeah. And lots of it. Someone made a quick and dramatic appearance change. We need to get an immediate mock-up done of Cole Shipley without the longer hair and possibly without the beard. Because we've likely been looking for the wrong damn guy all night."

TWENTY

They were nearly four hours down the road, headed south toward the Colorado state border, when Cole finally had to pull off somewhere and gas up the van. Lisa sat in the passenger seat next to him. Once they were clear of the valley, Cole had felt it was safe to have his wife join him up front. But she mostly just stared out the window into darkness. Because their daughter was in the back, they'd decided to wait until they were in private again to openly discuss their situation. Which meant a painfully long and quiet car ride. Jade had been relentless in bugging them for the truth. But Cole refused to have that conversation until he'd first talked with Lisa about it. Every word they told her right now carried incredible weight. Jade finally gave up and was currently asleep on one of the beanbag chairs with a blanket pulled over her. When fifty miles had turned into a hundred, and then two hundred, everyone had begun to breathe a little easier. They'd managed to escape immediate danger. Cole could only hope the FBI were still operating with the belief they were hiding somewhere in the valley. He wanted as much runway as possible before law enforcement began to expand their search. If he could somehow make it into Mexico before that happened, Cole felt confident they would be in the clear.

But they still had a long way to go.

He turned into a Loaf'N Jug twenty-four-hour gas station in the small town of Alamosa, Colorado, which was still about thirty-five miles from the New Mexico border. It was 2:38 in the morning. The parking lot was completely empty except for a rusted yellow Volkswagen Beetle parked over in the corner. It probably belonged to a gas station employee. Cole had his choice of gas pumps. He selected one on the farthest edge of the parking lot to avoid a direct view from inside the gas station.

"You want anything from inside?" he asked Lisa.

"Waters. And please be quick."

"That's the plan."

He got out, circled the van, and hurried toward the gas station. As he approached, he spotted a college-age guy with long black hair sitting on a stool behind the front counter. He looked like he was working alone. At first glance, Cole saw no other people inside the gas station. He entered the store and plopped a fifty-dollar bill down on the counter. The clerk had his eyes glued to a laptop. The kid had a dragon tattoo on his neck and piercings in both his nose and lip, and reeked of marijuana.

"Gas on pump nine," he said.

"You got it," said the clerk, not even looking up.

Cole would be paying cash from here on out. He had $5,000 stuffed inside one of the duffel bags. Credit cards were not an option—they could obviously be tracked. He would get new cards under their new names once they got settled, but the cash should be plenty to get them to their destination and hold them over until they got their feet beneath them. It felt surreal for him to even be thinking about Sayulita, Mexico. They had just left their whole life behind. And they were about to start a new life in a foreign country. How hard would it be to find a place to live? What would he do for work? Where would Jade go to school? Would they be able to find a good spine surgeon for Jade in Mexico?

These questions and countless others had been flooding his brain the past four hours on the open road. When they'd initially fled from

Austin thirteen years ago, Mexico had been an option they'd put on the table, and they'd even discussed Sayulita. It felt much safer than staying in the United States, where they might be more easily recognized. But they'd ultimately made the decision to stay stateside because of Jade, whom they wanted to have as normal a childhood as possible. It took them three years to find a normal home, and the longest they stayed in one place during that time was three months. They initially drove to Billings, Montana, where they paid cash for a weekly-rate motel. They mostly stayed in their room those first two weeks, monitoring the news. From there, they began bouncing from one small town to the next throughout Montana, Idaho, and Wyoming, and Cole had eventually started taking part-time jobs to make ends meet. Home Depot. Ace Hardware. Lowe's. It was difficult, both financially and emotionally. They stayed hyperalert and remained withdrawn from any relationships with outsiders. It wasn't until they landed in Winter Park that Cole decided to get a full-time job. But he still chose something with a low profile. A career with a corporation and any real future—like he used to have—had never been an option. He couldn't risk his face showing up somewhere more prominent. So they'd mostly lived month-to-month for thirteen years.

Cole left the store and walked back over to the van. The gas pumps were well lit, which made him feel exposed and vulnerable. He pulled a hose from the pump and stuck the nozzle into the van. As the gas started flowing, he glanced at the street they'd just exited. A lowrider car with rap music blaring and what looked like two teenagers with backward ball caps in the front seats slowly drove past. Cole made sure to stay out of view. He wanted as few eyes on him as possible. The gas pump was excruciatingly slow. He spotted more headlights approaching from up the road. As they got closer, Cole felt his heart begin to race. A police car. It paused at a streetlight about forty yards away. Cole pressed his back against the van, as to not be seen. If the police officer decided to pay the gas station a visit, he wasn't sure what he would do. He'd be a sitting duck. The gas finally finished pumping, but Cole didn't move.

At the moment, he was completely out of sight of the police car. But he would have to step back into full view to return the gas hose to the pump.

Cole peeked around the van. The police car was just sitting there at the intersection, even though the light was clearly green. What was the officer doing? Looking his way? Running his plates? Cole felt his fingers shaking. What if the police car suddenly pulled in directly behind him? Another quick peek. Then he let out a deep exhale as the police officer finally drove through the intersection and farther on down the road.

After returning the gas hose, Cole hurried back to the building. He stepped through the glass doors and moved straight to the back. He grabbed three water bottles from one of the fridges and a bag of Jade's favorite gummy worms, then quickly headed to the counter. The clerk pecked away on a computer to tally up his items. Cole glanced behind the counter, where he saw four small security camera TV monitors. Only two of them seemed to be operational. Both working security cameras showed views inside the store. His face was center position on one monitor. No cameras seemed to be working in the parking lot.

Cole paid and then glanced at the kid's laptop. "You connected to the internet here?"

"Yep. Otherwise, I'd be bored as hell all night."

"I'll give you a hundred bucks if you give me five minutes with your laptop."

The clerk pitched his head. "Seriously, dude?"

"Yes. I just need to check something online really quick, and my phone is dead. I'll use it right here at the counter." Cole counted out five twenty-dollar bills. "What do you say?"

"Yeah, man, cool. I could use the extra cash."

The clerk grabbed his laptop and placed it in front of Cole. He then took the hundred dollars and stuffed it in his blue jean pocket.

"Take your time, man," he said. "I'll just be over here on my phone."

Cole watched as the clerk stepped out from behind the counter and walked over to the corner of the store next to the ICEE machines. He quickly lit up a joint and began puffing away. Working quickly, Cole opened a new browser window and typed in a web address he hadn't accessed in a while. He thought it smarter to do this on someone else's computer than his burner phone right now. The site was off the grid and well secured. It was a simple storage website. There was only one video file listed, and he'd placed it there more than thirteen years ago. He clicked on it and watched as the video loaded onto the laptop screen. It had been captured from one of his home security cameras on the night they'd left town. He held his breath and pressed play. The video came from a security camera mounted under the corner of their roof and was focused directly on the front sidewalk and their street. At first, the video showed a calm, well-lit sidewalk. The time stamp on the video said 12:14 a.m., April 18. A white Toyota Corolla suddenly appeared at the curb. Then Jade's biological mother got out of the vehicle. She wore a black tank top and red micro shorts and was barefoot. Her hair was a mess, her makeup smeared. And she had a distraught look on her face. She hurried toward their front door and was in and out of camera view within a couple of seconds. Cole didn't have to see the rest to know what happened next. He would never stop having nightmares about it.

The woman had fallen straight into him. She was bleeding out from the midsection and gasping for her life. She claimed someone was coming for Jade. And she begged Cole with her last dying breath to save her daughter. At that point, Cole had scrambled back to the bedroom, woken up Lisa, and frantically told her what had happened. Trembling, they'd grabbed Jade from her crib and raced down the hallway toward the garage. Lisa had shrieked at the sight of the woman's dead body lying on the hardwood floor in the foyer as blood puddled beneath her. Jade began crying as they hurried into their three-car garage, still in their pajamas, climbed into their Lexus SUV, and pulled out.

They didn't even take time to strap Jade into her carrier and lock it into the car seat base. Lisa just held her tightly in her arms as they sped out of their neighborhood. They were only three minutes away from the house, sitting at a stop sign, when Cole had gotten a motion alert on his phone from the front door security camera. He'd immediately opened the security app and stared at the face of a stocky, late-twenties man with a beard, wearing a denim button-down, blue jeans, and cowboy boots at their front door. The man had briskly opened the unlocked door and disappeared inside.

Cole didn't possess the front door security footage. That night, he'd quickly tried to save all security videos from his home server on his phone. He had managed to download the corner roof footage showing Candace appearing on the front sidewalk followed by the mystery guy a few minutes later. However, someone had deleted all other footage before he could get to it. Cole figured it was the work of the intruder, who wanted to immediately cover his tracks. The guy must've known how to access their home system by using the digital pad on their kitchen wall.

Cole paused the video, squinted at the laptop screen. He had a good shot of the guy approaching up the sidewalk toward his front door. He'd been under so much duress earlier, upon discovering they'd been found by the FBI, that he'd been wondering if his mind had been playing tricks on him. Was it actually the same man earlier in the alley as in the video? But watching now confirmed he wasn't imagining it. The man on the video was definitely the same one who'd shot the policeman in the alley and then tried to also shoot him. Cole zoomed in on the video and could clearly see the same small tattoo on the man's right hand. He pressed play again and watched as the stocky guy disappeared from view. Cole had no idea what happened inside the house next. But he'd put the pieces together when the story broke the next morning: the guy had set them up for the fall.

Cole reflected on the terrifying moments after they'd watched the live security feed while sitting in their SUV. They'd wrestled immensely with what to do next. The practical side of them had screamed to immediately call the police and tell them what had just happened. But the emotional side had them absolutely paralyzed. Jade's mother was already dead. There was nothing they could do to save her. And Cole knew if they called the police, Jade would be instantly snatched away from them by child protective services. There was no way CPS would allow her to remain with Cole and Lisa, considering the horrific situation inside their home. That thought had scared the hell out of them. They had no idea what had just happened to her mother, but they certainly believed Candace's claims that Jade was not safe and needed to be rescued from whatever situation had developed. If they handed Jade over to CPS, they might be putting her right back in danger. There was no way they were going to do that.

So they chose not to do anything until they spoke with their attorney and got his legal guidance. They knew the matter with Jade needed to be handled with the utmost care and caution, especially because it would undoubtedly involve the courts again. They wanted to legally protect both Jade and themselves. They certainly didn't want to risk a second chance at becoming her real parents. But that opportunity never came. Their lawyer hadn't answered their multiple calls that night and didn't immediately return their frantic voicemails. By early the next morning, their whole world was rocked, as their faces began showing up on every local media outlet with the most staggering headlines.

Local couple suspected of murdering 21-year-old mother and kidnapping her 9-month-old baby girl

TWENTY-ONE

Jade jolted awake. She was breathing hard and even sweating. For a moment, she felt relieved. It was just a nightmare. It wasn't real. The frightened look on her mom's face when telling her they had to immediately leave the house. The scrambling to pack a travel bag. The hiding on top of Rendezvous Mountain watching police cars parked outside their home. Her dad getting his head shaved. Evading police stops while listening to her mom pray they could somehow get away safely. All of it.

But as her eyes slowly adjusted in the dark, she realized she was not in her bed at home. She could feel the beanbag beneath her. She could make out the multiple duffel bags. The truth hit her hard and again stole her breath. This was real. She was in the back of an old van. She put a trembling hand to her mouth to keep herself from crying. What was happening? Why were her parents in trouble? Why was the FBI trying to find them?

She'd fallen asleep to these questions, and now they were right back in front of her. She trusted her parents, but this was impossible for her to process. Her thoughts immediately shifted to Tyler, as they'd been doing throughout the night. What was he thinking right now? He'd probably been texting her all night and wondering why she hadn't responded. He might be sitting there thinking he'd done something wrong. That she no longer liked him for some reason. It broke her heart because this couldn't be further from the truth. She needed to somehow let him know what had happened. That she was okay, and her silence wasn't his fault. But she felt helpless. Her mom had destroyed her phone.

Then she noticed her mom's purse sitting on the van floor next to the duffel bags at her feet. Was her mom's new phone inside it? Jade glanced up front. She knew her mom had moved into the passenger seat at some point during the drive. She could see the back of her shoulder poking out from the seat. They were stopped somewhere. She peered straight through the windshield. Gas station? Her dad was not currently in the driver's seat. She scooted off the beanbag, pulled her mom's purse over toward her, and began quietly reaching around inside it. She felt her mom's wallet, a hairbrush, a set of keys . . . and then her fingers wrapped around a familiar device.

Jade pulled it out. The phone. Not her mom's usual phone but one she'd begun using earlier that night. Jade could feel her adrenaline kick into high gear and her heart rate pick up speed. If she was going to do this, she had to get moving. Her dad would probably be back soon. She stuck the phone in the back pocket of her blue jeans. Then she eased up into the gap between the cargo area and the front seats.

"Where are we?" she said.

Her mom glanced over. "Hey. You get some sleep?"

"A little."

"We're getting gas."

"Are we still in Colorado?"

"Yes. A town called Alamosa."

"Oh. Well, I really need to go to the bathroom."

"Okay, but be super quick. Your dad just went inside to pay."

"I'll be quick."

Jade pulled on the handle in the back and slid the big van door open. She climbed out, shut it behind her, and glanced around. If her dad was inside the gas station, she wasn't going in there. He'd probably kill her if he found what she was doing. But she had to talk to Tyler.

It was so cruel to just disappear on him without a word. She had no idea when she would see him again. She was determined to keep their relationship going, even if she had to do it from a distance. But the thought of that made her want to cry again.

Jade stepped around the gas pumps, slowly moved toward the building. She could now see her dad standing up near the front counter. He was staring down. What was he doing? It looked like he was working on a laptop or something. She didn't see a gas station employee anywhere. After taking another deep breath, Jade veered off toward the side of the building. She turned a corner and stepped into a dark part of the parking lot that was blocked from the main lights. Her heart racing, she pulled the phone from her back pocket. The phone screen was unlocked. Her mom hadn't set up a security code. Not that it would've stopped her—her mom always used Jade's birthday as her passcode. The phone was nothing fancy, which was fine. She just needed to make a phone call.

She began pecking out the numbers with her thumb. Her dad had threatened to confiscate her phone last week for not finishing a school assignment, so she'd memorized Tyler's phone number in case she had to reach him from one of her friends' phones. She pressed "Call." It was nearly three in the morning. Would he even be awake? Would he answer a phone call this late from a random number? When the phone got to the fourth ring, she found herself audibly begging for him to answer.

Please! Please! And then he did. Thank God.

"Uh . . . hello?"

He sounded like he'd been sleeping.

"Tyler, it's me," she whispered, her voice spiking.

"Jade?"

"Yes!"

He was alert now. "Are you okay? I've been texting you all night."

"I'm so sorry. I don't have my phone. It's been an insane night!"

"For me, too! The FBI came to my house earlier asking about you."

Jade gasped. Why would the FBI talk to Tyler? He was just a kid like her.

"What did they say?" she asked.

"They said you were in danger."

"Really? I'm okay. But my parents are acting so crazy. We had to dodge the police earlier and get out of there for some reason."

"Where are you now?"

"Some random town called Alamosa, I think. We're at a Loaf'N Jug getting gas. This is my mom's phone. I had to sneak off with it to call you. But I *had* to talk to you."

"I'm so glad you did. I've been freaking out."

"Me too."

"So you really don't know what's going on?"

"No, my parents won't tell me *anything*. It's so weird."

"Where are y'all going?"

Jade sighed. "You'll never believe this. We're going to Mexico. They are planning to drive all the way to some beach town called Sayulita. I've never even heard of it."

"What? For how long?"

"I don't know. Hopefully not too long. Because I'm already missing you."

"I'm missing you, too."

TWENTY-TWO

Burns and his crew rented hotel rooms at a place called the Viking Lodge near the center of Winter Park. When they'd arrived in town four hours earlier, he'd had no plans to stay. He had thought he'd be throwing his handcuffed fugitives into the back of the Tahoe and driving them to the Denver office for questioning and processing. But his plans had certainly changed. It was nearing three in the morning now, and most of his guys had already called it a night. He'd told them to get quick sleep, because he needed them ready to go again by sunrise. But Burns himself was still awake and sitting at a table in a small conference room they'd set up as their local war room. There was zero chance he was going to be able to sleep tonight. Davis sat across the table from him and was currently on the phone with the Granby Police Department. His right-hand man had rebuffed his orders to go get some rest. Burns appreciated it. He needed someone there to bounce his random thoughts off.

Another agent, Myers, was also in the war room with them. A wiry, late-twenties guy with thick black glasses, he sat at the end of the table, wearing headphones in front of a laptop. Myers was a tech genius whose role in this operation was monitoring various phones, emails, and social media they'd tagged as those of interest earlier in the evening. Burns almost hadn't brought Myers with him, thinking it was unnecessary. He was certainly glad he had now that things had gone haywire. The conference table was littered with reports, coffee cups, and candy wrappers. It had already been a long night. Burns was reviewing a big stack of interview transcripts from concertgoers. He was looking for any nuggets that might help him put some pieces together. But his eyes were starting to get blurry.

Davis hung up, sighed, and said, "Gilley's son is worthless, boss. They can't keep him awake long enough to ask him any questions. It's probably going to take until morning to get him to sober up enough to be somewhat sensible. I'm not counting on him being helpful."

Burns sighed. They'd finally managed to track down Jethro Gilley's son, who ran the day-to-day operations at the storage property where Cole Shipley was a renter. He'd been passed out in the back of a friend's truck in the middle of a campground. As Gilley's father had suspected, his son was way too drunk to be useful to them. Granby Police currently had him over at their station and were trying every remedy they could think of to quickly sober him up.

"What about other renters around Cole's slip?" Burns asked.

They still had two agents out there knocking on doors and waking people.

"They've talked to two of them. One guy couldn't remember a thing. Said he barely ever used his boat anymore. It's just been sitting there, rusting out, for years. The other guy thought it might've been a gray minivan. Or white. He wasn't too sure on make or model."

"Great. Let's pull over every soccer mom in a minivan starting tomorrow morning."

"They're still at it, boss. Someone must know something."

Burns dropped a report on the table, rubbed his face in his hands. He couldn't believe this was happening right now. They'd had the Shipleys dead to rights. This should have all been over by now. Instead of sitting in this room with Davis and Myers, he should've been sitting with Cole and Lisa. With a satisfied grin on his face. He should have been working with the FBI's public relations and media team, getting ready to break the big news that two of the most wanted fugitives on their list had finally been arrested. He felt like he was having flashbacks to thirteen years ago, when Cole had inexplicably managed to stay a step ahead, even with the full force of the FBI in pursuit. Burns had known then that Cole was an incredibly smart guy. And he'd clearly remained prepared all these years. So what was their plan? Where were they going to go if all this blew up on them? With each passing hour, Burns grew more concerned they were already gone from the valley.

Myers suddenly started snapping his fingers wildly at the end of the table.

Burns perked up, looked over. Davis did the same.

Yanking his headphones off, Myers punched a volume button on his laptop.

"We got a hit!" he announced. "The daughter! She's on the phone right now with that Healey kid."

Burns had a judge on standby tonight to swiftly issue wiretap orders and warrants. It might have just paid off in a big way. He suddenly heard the voice of a teenage girl through the laptop's speaker. He then recognized the voice of Tyler Healey, the boyfriend they'd spoken with earlier in the night. He bolted to his feet, moved closer to the laptop, hanging on every word.

"Where are you now?" Tyler asked.

"Some random town called Alamosa, I think. We're at a Loaf'N Jug getting gas. This is my mom's phone. I had to sneak off with it to call you. But I had to talk to you."

"I'm so glad you did. I've been freaking out."

"Me too."

"So you really don't know what's going on?"

"No, my parents won't tell me anything. It's so weird."

"Where are y'all going?"

"You'll never believe this. We're going to Mexico. They are planning to drive all the way to some beach town called Sayulita. I've never even heard of it."

Burns turned to Davis. "Get someone to that gas station ASAP!"

Davis already had his phone to his ear. "On it!"

TWENTY-THREE

Cole shut the clerk's laptop. Twenty-four hours after they'd bolted from Austin that night, he'd created an anonymous email account and sent the home security video of Candace McGee and the mysterious guy to his attorney. Cole had claimed their innocence and asked their attorney to share the video with the FBI. The attorney had responded within a few hours, telling him he'd turned the video over, but it had changed little. The Feds still had a murder weapon with his fingerprints on it. The attorney said the only way for them to prove their innocence was to immediately turn themselves in. The longer they hid, the guiltier they looked, which made his job even harder. Cole and Lisa found themselves in the exact same desperate spot. On the run. Willing to sacrifice their lives in order to protect Jade.

Cole motioned for the kid that he was finished. Then he stepped out of the gas station with his grocery items in a plastic bag. He needed to tell Lisa the truth about the stocky guy. But he certainly didn't want Jade knowing anything about it. He had to protect her emotionally from an even scarier reality. If they could get to Mexico by the end of the day, the truth wouldn't even matter. This time he would make sure no one would ever find them again. They would go so far off the grid. He paused on the front sidewalk. He could hear someone talking. But there were still no other cars in the parking lot. He moved down the sidewalk toward where the voice was coming. He could hear it more clearly now. A girl. And not just any girl. Jade. He cursed. His daughter was talking to someone on the phone.

He rushed forward, turned the corner, spotted her huddled in the dark, her back to him, a phone pressed to her ear. Everything inside him wanted to scream at her. They had clearly told her no phones. Not until they settled somewhere, which might take several weeks. It was too risky. The Feds could already be monitoring the phones of everyone they knew in town. But he knew lashing out at his daughter right now was unwise. She was fragile. He tried to be understanding. She had of course looked for an opportunity to make a phone call. She was confused and scared to death. And from the sound of it, she was on the phone with her boyfriend, Tyler. Would the FBI already know about that relationship?

Cole took a deep breath to try to settle himself, stepped closer toward her, and cleared his throat to get her attention.

Jade spun around, her eyes widening, her mouth frozen open.

"I need you to hang up, baby," he said as calmly as he could. "Tell him goodbye and then give me the phone, okay?"

Jade swallowed. Into the phone, she said, "I have to go, Tyler."

Then she hung up, handed the phone to him. Her eyes immediately watered. "I'm so sorry, Daddy," she said, crying harder by the second.

He stuck the phone in his pocket, dropped the plastic bag, and wrapped his arms around her. "Baby, it's okay. I understand. We've asked a lot of you tonight. I get that. And you've been incredibly brave. But we can't be calling our friends right now. I know that sucks. Especially for you with Tyler. I'm sorry. But we just can't do it."

She pulled away slightly. "When will I be able to talk to him again?"

He pressed his lips together. "I don't know."

The answer was *never*, but he couldn't bear telling her that right now.

Her emotional state immediately flipped on him. Her sobbing stopped, and she instead glared at him with narrowed eyes and her nostrils flaring. "This isn't fair, Dad! You can't just take me away from Tyler and all my friends. I didn't do anything wrong!"

"I know," he agreed. "You're right. It's not fair."

"It's not fair to Tyler, either," she continued. "The FBI was at his house tonight."

Cole stiffened. "What?"

"He said they were asking about me and about us."

Panic seized him. The Feds already knew about Tyler. "Did he tell them anything?"

"He doesn't know anything, Dad!"

Cole's mind was swirling. The FBI could be monitoring the boy's phone. Which meant they could be currently tracing the location of his daughter's phone call.

"We have to go!" he said to Jade, his eyes flashing.

She crossed her arms in defiance. "I'm not leaving until you start telling me the truth."

"I can't right now."

"You keep saying that. Then I'm not going *anywhere*."

Cole thought about the police officer who'd just driven by the gas station a few minutes ago. He was nearby. All it would take was one quick phone call from the FBI for the officer to zip right back over. They had to run.

"Jade, I'm sorry."

She remained rigid. "Sorry for what? Screwing up my life?"

"No, for this," he said, reaching down and lifting her over his shoulder. He spun around and hustled back over to the van. Jade was yelling and hitting him on the back the whole way, which caused Lisa to pop out of the van.

"What the heck is going on?" she asked.

"Get the van door open," he instructed. "We have to get away from here right now. And our daughter is not cooperating!"

Lisa reached up and pulled open the van door, and Cole set Jade down inside.

"Did something happen?" Lisa asked.

"Yes!" Jade yelled. "Dad is acting like a lunatic! I'm going to jump out!"

Cole turned to Lisa. "Get in there with her and stop her from being an idiot. I'll explain when we get on the road."

Lisa climbed into the back, tried to get Jade to calm down. But their daughter only continued to lash out at them. Cole slammed the door shut behind him and swiftly circled the vehicle. Realizing he still had the burner phone Jade had just used, he pulled it from his pocket, reared back, and tossed it across the parking lot. He then reached into his other pocket, pulled out his own burner, and did the same. The two phones could somehow be tied together through his store purchase a few months ago. He couldn't take any chances. He would pick up new phones somewhere along the way. He climbed behind the wheel, started the van, and stomped on the gas pedal. The van bounced through potholes in the parking lot before reentering the street.

Cole was only fifty yards from the gas station when he saw a police car in his rearview mirror with its red and blue lights blinking. He gripped his steering wheel tightly, wondered if he was about to go on a high-speed chase. But thankfully the police car pulled into the same gas station parking lot they'd just left. His panic now exploded. The Feds *were* listening. The FBI knew exactly where they were at this very moment. He pushed the gas pedal to the floor and crossed a bridge over the Rio Grande into the middle of town. He spotted more red and blue lights up ahead, coming straight toward them. Cole quickly turned onto the next street, pulled into an alley between a dry cleaner and a liquor store, and turned off his headlights. He could feel his heart in his throat as he watched his mirrors, wondering if he'd made the right choice. Seconds later, a police car pulled onto the same street as them, but quickly passed by the dark alley without noticing them.

Cole exhaled, but his chest felt so tight. The police car was clearly coming after them. Because there were so few cars on the road at this hour, the police were probably going to start stopping everyone they encountered in hopes of finding them. And Alamosa was no small town—he guessed around ten thousand people—which meant they had a significant police presence. There were likely more police officers out and about right now beginning to circle the streets looking for moving headlights.

"What is happening, Cole?" Lisa said from the back. "Why are there so many police cars all of a sudden?"

"They know we're here," he admitted.

"What? How?"

"We made a mistake, Lisa. They're tracking our phones. That's why I got rid of them."

He glanced at his daughter in the rearview mirror. She no longer looked angry. Her face was sunken with guilt. There was no reason to beat her up about it.

"Did you call someone?" Lisa yelled at him. "Are you crazy?"

"Doesn't matter," he said. "We just have to get out of here."

He slowly backed out of the alley but kept the headlights off. Pausing, he searched both ways up and down the street. No sign of the cops. While it was dark out, Cole had just enough surrounding street-light to make several more turns, which he swiftly did. He was back on the main street, driving with his headlights off. His speedometer hit sixty and then seventy. New headlights up ahead. Cole quickly pulled off the street again and stopped in a small parking lot in front of an auto mechanic, which had a dozen other cars parked out front. This time, it wasn't a police vehicle. It was a black Jeep Wrangler. When it passed, he pulled back into the street and floored it again. He passed by several more retail strips and followed the signs leading them out to Highway 285, which would take them south into New Mexico. As they left the lights of the inner city, the streets grew darker, so he was forced to turn on his headlights again. Once on 285, his foot grew even heavier on the gas pedal. They hit eighty miles per hour, which started to make the van vibrate a bit. But he didn't slow down until Alamosa had completely disappeared in his rearview mirror.

Lisa remained agitated. "Do the police know we're in this van?"

"I don't think so. The security cameras weren't working at the gas station."

"What about the clerk? Can he identify it?"

Cole had intentionally parked out of view from the front counter. Plus, he'd never once noticed the young guy look out the front windows. The kid had been too absorbed in video games on his laptop and messing with his phone. "I think we're okay."

"You *think*?" Lisa said, her voice continuing to rise with anger. "I can't believe this, Cole. You're the one always telling me to be so careful. And then you blew it? Who did you call?"

"Stop, Mom!" Jade interrupted, crying again. "It wasn't Dad! It was me! I called Tyler. I'm sorry. I didn't know this would happen. This is all my fault. I screwed everything up!"

Realizing her misguided anger, Lisa quickly changed her tone. "No, baby, you didn't screw anything up. None of this is your fault. We don't ever want you to think that."

"She's right," Cole agreed. "If anyone is to blame, it's me."

He kept thinking about the money. If he hadn't touched it, they would still be sleeping peacefully in their beds back home. He'd allowed his own brokenness about his daughter's dire medical condition to cloud his better judgment.

"No one is to blame," Lisa clarified. "We're all in this together."

Jade continued to sob, her whole body shaking. Lisa pulled her in close, held her, and Cole saw tears now forming in his wife's eyes. She looked up at him in the mirror and mouthed, *I'm sorry.* Sitting there, watching his girls lose it, Cole felt his heart ripping in two. All he wanted to do was protect them. And he was failing miserably.

TWENTY-FOUR

Brock Gunner was slouched behind the steering wheel of his Ford Bronco loaner, having difficulty staying awake, when he got the text. It was a few minutes past three in the morning. He'd been parked for the past two hours in an empty lot behind the Grand Park Community Recreation Center, which was a half mile from the Shipleys' home. He hadn't bothered trying to find a bed anywhere since he needed to be able to instantly respond to anything that popped up during the night. The last report he got was that one of the Shipleys' vehicles had been found at a storage property over in Granby, but there were still no leads on their actual whereabouts. The police continued to have all exits from the valley manned and guarded. At this point, Brock thought everyone, including Cole and Lisa Shipley and their daughter, might have buckled down for the night.

Where are you?

He responded: Still here in Winter Park.

Well, they're not. They pulled a Houdini and somehow made it out of the valley. They're already four hours down the road.

Brock cursed. Where?

FBI traced a call from the daughter to a town called Alamosa.

Brock slammed his fist against his steering wheel. They arrest them already?

No, they got away. Feds are headed there now.

They know what they're driving yet?

No, still haven't figured it out.

Brock searched his mapping app. Alamosa was 222 miles south. He texted: I can be in Alamosa in three hours.

They're probably already gone. Daughter told boyfriend they're going to Mexico. Closest border crossing is El Paso.

I have border patrol contacts there.

Call Justin. Get on the plane and get down there ASAP.

TWENTY-FIVE

An FBI helicopter arrived from Denver within an hour of Burns and his team tracing the phone call. It was one of the FBI's light utility choppers that could travel up to 175 miles per hour. With the Shipleys now out on the open road, Burns needed to be able to cover a lot of ground as fast as possible. The helicopter landed in a parking lot right next to the Viking Lodge and likely startled awake vacationers staying in other hotel rooms. Burns, Davis, and Agent Myers quickly boarded. The pilot had them up in the air within sixty seconds and began racing across a dark sky toward Alamosa, Colorado.

So far, there had been no confirmation from the Alamosa County Sheriff's Office that the Shipleys had been apprehended. But he'd been getting regular updates. The store clerk and security footage both confirmed Cole had been inside the gas station. But the clerk said he never saw the vehicle he was driving. And the exterior security cameras were all down. The sheriff's office was trying to find other security cameras in proximity that might have caught sight of a vehicle coming or going around the same time.

Agent Myers had been able to track the specific phone the daughter had used to place the call to Tyler Healey. According to their GPS tracking map, the device was still located somewhere near the gas station. Burns guessed Cole had dumped it. It was clear from the brief exchange he'd overheard between Cole and his daughter he was not pleased she'd used the phone. Burns found it ironic his fugitive was dealing with the same kinds of frustrating daughter issues he was. Neither of them had any control over their teenager.

They finally landed in an open field right next to the gas station around five thirty in the morning. It was still dark outside. There were two police vehicles in the parking lot. Burns, Davis, and Myers all climbed out of the chopper and hurried over to the building. A sturdy fiftysomething man in a tan police uniform with a matching cowboy hat met them at the front of the store.

"Sheriff Lewis," he introduced himself.

They shook hands. Burns had spoken on the phone with him several times already.

"Anything new?" Burns asked.

"Nothing. We still don't know what the hell we're looking for out there."

"So no luck with other area security cameras?"

"Not yet. This is a safe town. Not a lot of store owners feel the need to put up security cameras. I should take that as a compliment, I guess. We'll keep checking around. As we discussed earlier, we put up a checkpoint on 285 within minutes of you first alerting us to the situation. We've had maybe a dozen vehicles pass through there the past two hours. But nobody matching the descriptions you gave us."

"How many other ways to get south other than 285?"

"Honestly, dozens."

"Figured. They probably fled town before you even got it set up."

"Maybe. But I've had a dozen officers out there looking. Plus, we called over to La Jara, Monte Vista, and the Costilla County Sheriff's Office to get them all up to speed."

"Thank you, Sheriff."

"One last thing." He held up two matching phones in a sealed plastic bag. "We found both near the dumpsters at the edge of the parking lot a few minutes ago. I presume one of them is the phone you've been tracking here."

"Most likely." Burns turned to Myers. "See if we have a match."

The sheriff handed over the phones. He turned, nodded toward the inside of the station. "Hate to be the bearer of bad news, Agent Burns, but that clerk in there is about as clueless as a rock. I know him. His name is Johnny and he's completely baked. His dad has been in and out of my jail many times. Mostly minor stuff. Not sure he'll be much help."

"Appreciate the insight."

"You bet. I'll be out here if you need me."

Burns and his crew went inside the building. The young clerk was situated behind the front counter, watching them closely, fidgeting nervously while shifting his weight back and forth. Johnny was clearly not comfortable around the police. There was no telling what the kid might have stashed in a backpack somewhere.

Burns introduced himself and the others and then instructed Myers to work on the security system behind the counter. The agent quickly brought up camera footage showing Cole enter the store earlier, grab some items, and approach the counter. As expected, his head was now bald, and the beard was completely gone. He paid, and then, after a brief exchange, the clerk handed over his laptop.

"Why did he want your laptop?" Burns asked the kid.

Johnny shrugged. "He offered me a hundred bucks, so I let him borrow it. Didn't ask any questions. I checked the browser history after the SWAT team arrived and scared the hell out of me. The guy only went to one website and spent about five minutes on there."

"Show us," Burns said.

Johnny grabbed his laptop from a back counter and set it in front of them. Myers came around to share in the viewing. They all huddled close as the clerk pulled up his browser history and then clicked on a website that had a set of random letters as the web address. A new web page opened that showed only a black screen with three empty text boxes situated directly in the middle.

"What kind of website is that?" Davis asked.

"Looks like a secure server," Myers replied.

"Can you get in?" Davis asked him.

"I'll give it my best shot."

Myers pulled the laptop in front of him and started pecking away at the keyboard.

Burns turned back to the clerk. "What exactly did this guy say to you?"

Another shrug. "Like I told the sheriff, not much. Said he needed to jump online for a few minutes and that his phone was dead. That was it, I swear. When he was finished, he left without another word."

"And you really saw *nothing* in the parking lot?" Davis asked.

"Sorry, dude. I mean, sir. I wasn't paying attention. I just kinda get lost in my own world in here in the middle of the night."

Burns glanced around the station. When he'd first heard about Cole using the clerk's laptop, he figured his fugitive was just checking the news to try to stay a step ahead of their pursuit. But that didn't appear to be the case at all. So what could Cole have stored on a secured server that he felt he had to access right now in the middle of being hunted? Hopefully Myers would have the answer to that question shortly.

They caught a ride in the back of a police cruiser over to the Alamosa County Sheriff's Office, where they tried desperately to find *something* that would help aid them in their pursuit of Cole and Lisa. After an hour or so, they finally got their first major break. But it didn't come from their stop in Alamosa; it came from Winter Park. Burns was standing in a small conference room with Myers sitting at a table and working on a laptop in front of him when Davis rushed into the room holding up his phone.

"Boss, got a Deputy Richards here on the phone. He was working the checkpoint for the Berthoud Pass last night." Davis spoke into the phone. "I got you on speaker now, Deputy. Can you tell Agent Burns what you just told me?"

"Yes, sir. So, like I said, I was manning the checkpoint for the pass last night, turning everyone back. An old white van came up with a guy sitting in front. Probably in his forties. But he didn't look anything like the fugitive we'd been searching for. He said he was a plumber. I recognized the name of the plumbing company printed on the van.

Anyway, I didn't think anything of it until this morning, when I more closely examined the new mock-up of Cole Shipley you guys sent out late last night. I'm certain it was the same guy."

"How certain?" Burns asked.

"Ninety percent. Shaved head, no beard, same facial features and eyes."

"Did you search the van?" Burns asked.

"No, sir. I mean, I should have in hindsight. But like I said, I recognized the plumbing company. The old man who started it was a friend of my dad's. So I just stupidly assumed. Not my best police work. But there were *a lot* of cars in that line."

Burns growled in frustration, shook his head.

"What can you tell us about the van?" Davis asked.

"White Ford. Probably twenty years old. Looked a little run-down. *Gunderson Family Plumbers* was on the side in blue. It was faded but legible. I called Teddy Gunderson a few minutes ago. He said he sold off his vans a decade ago, when he shut down his company. You can still find photos of the vehicles online."

"And you saw no one else in the van?" Davis asked.

"No, sir."

Burns asked, "Anything else you can tell us about the guy that might help?"

"Not much. But I'll give him credit. He was smooth. Never flinched. Seemed totally relaxed sitting there and talking to me. Made up a helluva story on the spot about how disgusting the back of the van was from a job he'd just come from. It was smart."

"All right," Davis said. "You think of anything else, you call us."

"Will do."

Davis hung up, held up his phone to show Burns. He'd already been searching for Gunderson Family Plumbers vans online. "Matches the description of some sort of white van one of the neighbors at the storage facility mentioned."

"Yeah, it does," Burns said, still shaking his head. "But, dammit, we had him. This should all be over right now. Ask the sheriff to help get that photo out to every police department from here on down to El Paso. And then call our pilot and tell him to get the chopper up and running. If they're headed that way, we're headed that way."

"I'm in," Myers suddenly announced.

They circled in behind him to examine his laptop screen.

"Not much to it," Myers said. "One short video. Nothing else."

"Play it," Burns instructed.

The agent pressed play, and Burns leaned in close. It was a home security video taken at night showing a front sidewalk and street. He immediately recognized it. It was thirteen-year-old footage from the night Cole Shipley had killed Candace McGee. The video showed the woman arriving at his home in the middle of the night, followed by a mystery man several minutes later. It was the only known security footage from the night in question. Everything else had been deleted from the home's security server.

"What is this?" Davis asked.

"A video Cole Shipley's lawyer sent to us the day after they disappeared back in Austin claiming his innocence. We investigated the man in the video but found nothing. We could never identify him and had no clue why he was also at the Shipley home that night. We thought maybe he somehow helped Cole. An accomplice. It's always bothered me. But because we had a murder weapon with Cole's fingerprints, and they ran, we continued to pursue them as the primary suspects."

"Interesting. Why would Cole stop here at this gas station, borrow this clerk's laptop, and pull up this video? Kind of random, don't you think?"

Burns pondered that a moment. "If I've learned anything about Cole Shipley, nothing he does is random. Everything is calculated. Maybe this guy is still helping him. We need to figure out who he is."

TWENTY-SIX

Cole pulled the van into the parking lot of the Cielo Vista Mall in El Paso around eleven the next morning. It was a gray day, and sprinkling. A thunderstorm hung in the distance. The remainder of the drive from Colorado, through New Mexico, and then into Texas, had been thankfully uneventful. No unexpected police traps. No car chases. No anxiety-fueled moments. Both Lisa and Jade had slept most of the way in the back of the van. Like him, they were physically and emotionally exhausted. While driving through the night, Cole had begun fantasizing about lying in a hammock on a warm Mexican beach and sleeping all day while the ocean breeze blew over him. They had endured some harsh winters while living in Colorado, and he looked forward to the dramatic change in weather. At least, that's what he kept telling himself in order to spin things positively in his own mind.

They'd almost made it. Within the hour, they should be across the border and hopefully home free. But first a quick stop to grab new burner phones while they were still in the United States. He wasn't sure he'd have great phone-purchasing options once they were inside Mexico and traveling through random small towns. He wanted them to be able to always communicate, especially in a country where they would need to quickly learn a new language. Plus, Cole wanted GPS mapping so he could follow the fastest and safest way to get to Sayulita. He didn't need to be driving off a jungle cliff somewhere.

He parked the van in between the mall and a separate Red Lobster restaurant situated in the mall parking lot, which stirred Lisa awake in the back. She popped up and quickly scooted next to him in between the seats.

"Where are we?" she asked, rubbing her eyes.

"El Paso."

"Wow, already? I must've been sleeping hard." She stared out the windshield. "Why are we parked in front of Red Lobster?"

"Thought you guys might want some shrimp and biscuits."

She frowned at him.

"Look to your right," he said.

She glanced over. "We're at a shopping mall?"

"I want to pick up new phones before we cross the border."

"Oh, okay." She peeked behind her. "She's been tossing, turning, and restless all night."

"This has been understandably traumatic for her."

"We need to tell her the truth, Cole. We can't continue to keep her in the dark, or she'll stop trusting us. We'll lose her."

"I know. I just want to protect her."

"She's tougher than you think."

"Yeah. I guess I still see a little girl reaching out with her tiny hands, wanting her daddy to pick her up and hold her. I wish we could've stayed in that place with her forever."

"Me too. Speaking of truth telling, what really happened with the gash on your arm?"

He swallowed. "I got shot," he whispered.

Her eyes went wide. "What?"

"Yeah. While I was in town trying to evade the FBI. I ran from a cop. But then something even more frightening happened I've been needing to tell you about."

He checked to make sure Jade was still fully asleep and then went on to quietly explain his traumatic encounter with the stocky guy in the alley, and how he'd confirmed it was the same man by reviewing the home security video he had kept. Lisa's mouth dropped open, and she cupped both hands in front of it.

"How is this even possible, Cole?"

"I have no idea."

"You could have been killed."

"I know."

"How did he find us? And why is he coming after you all these years later?"

"Questions I've been asking myself the past few hours. I can only think we're somehow a threat to someone. But I'm not sure how or why."

"We need to tell the FBI about him. He killed a cop. Maybe it could somehow help us."

"We tried that before, and it got us nowhere, remember?"

"Right. You're positive it was the same man?"

"One hundred percent. Seeing him up close and personal was surreal. But I didn't want to say anything in front of Jade that might scare her even more."

"Yeah, I'm okay leaving that part out—for now. But we still need to tell her the truth about everything else."

"Agreed. As soon as we get across the border, we'll stop and have that conversation."

"Okay."

"I need to go grab these phones now. Stay here."

Cole got out of the van, pulled the top of the gray hoodie he'd put on during the night over his head, and walked across the parking lot toward the two-story mall. He entered through the glass doors of a Dillard's department store and crossed through the various clothing, shoe, and makeup sections, until he found his way into the main mall corridor. The shopping mall was busy, but then he remembered it was still only Sunday. It felt like a full week had passed since they'd celebrated Jade's birthday in Grand Lake yesterday. He was grateful for all the extra faces around. It was easier to blend in and made him feel less exposed. Still, he kept the hood up to cover as much of his face as possible. He stopped at a mall map, spotted an electronics store on the upper level called Cellular Tech Works, and then made a beeline for the nearest escalator.

While ascending, he shook his head. It was hard to believe the plan had worked. All the years of preparation—purchasing the van, keeping it running, constantly updating supplies, clothes, cash, phones, fake passports—had actually paid off. It had been emotionally draining for him to stay in plan mode for the past ten years. But it had saved his family.

TWENTY-SEVEN

Jade jerked awake, opened her eyes, and then sighed with disappointment. Every time she'd woken up over the past few hours, she'd immediately prayed she'd be back in her bedroom and none of this would be real. And the only thing on her agenda for the day would be hanging out with Tyler. But each time reality hit, she felt devastated. She rubbed her face in her hands to try to wipe off the fog and then gradually moved up toward the front of the van. She could see it was raining outside. Her mom sat in the front passenger seat staring intently out the wet windows.

"Where are we?" Jade asked.

"El Paso. Your dad ran inside the mall to get new phones."

"Oh." Jade grimaced. Her back was really hurting. She felt it the most while lying stationary for an extended time. It had been frustrating waking up with aches up and down her back every morning before school. It would sometimes take a couple of hours to work it out to where she could focus in the classroom.

Her mom turned fully to face her. "You okay?"

"No. What's going to happen with my surgery now?"

Her mom sighed. "I don't know, honey. But we'll figure it out. I promise."

"Are we really going into Mexico?"

Not Our Daughter

"Yes."

"For how long?"

"I honestly don't know."

She huffed. "Nobody seems to know much of anything. And that just sucks."

"Yes, it does."

Jade was surprised how her mother's response lacked much positivity. Her mom had been mostly reassuring for a majority of the trip, but she seemed to be losing her optimism. Or maybe she was just tired. Since they were alone, Jade decided to press her for more information.

"What did Dad do, Mom? You can tell me."

Her mom looked at her. "What do you mean?"

"All of this? Everything that's happened. It's because of Dad, right?"

She shook her head. "No. Your dad is a wonderful man."

"So then, what, it's you? You caused this? The FBI is after you?"

"It's neither of us, Jade."

"Then why all the secrecy? Why won't you just tell me why this is happening?"

"Your dad and I were just talking about that. We plan to tell you everything as soon as we get into Mexico. I promise."

"But we have time right now. We're just sitting here doing nothing."

"I know. But your dad needs to be part of this conversation."

Jade huffed again, stared through the windshield at the Red Lobster in front of them. "Can I run inside the restaurant real quick and go to the restroom?"

Her mom glared at her. "Are you going to try to call Tyler again?"

"How? I don't have access to a phone."

"That didn't stop you before."

Jade rolled her eyes. "I'm just going to the restroom, that's all. I swear. You can come with me, if you want."

"No, I need to stay here and keep watch. Just hurry."

Jade pulled open the sliding door of the van, got out, and shut it behind her. She briskly walked toward the restaurant, weaving in and

133

out of about a dozen other vehicles, the sprinkling getting her wet. She stepped inside and asked a hostess about the restrooms. After getting directions, she crossed through the restaurant toward the back corner. About half the tables were already filled with early birds grabbing lunch. Most were gray-headed. A couple of other people sat on stools in the bar area. The food smelled good, even though she didn't care much for seafood. She'd eaten nothing but snacks since dinner last night and craved real food. After finding the restroom, she grabbed a stall, quickly took care of her business, washed her hands, and returned to the restaurant.

Jade froze next to the bar area in the middle that had several mounted TVs. A photo of her family was currently situated on the center screen. The sight of it shook her. She recognized the photo. It was one they'd had framed on their fireplace mantel—the three of them in Aspen last summer, standing on the sidewalk outside Hotel Jerome. She was still wearing her ugly braces. She moved closer to get a better look. The TV was tuned to a national news station. She spotted the logo in the corner. It looked like a press conference had just started. An older, heavyset, gray-bearded man wearing a cowboy hat and a black jacket stood behind a podium. A digital tag at the bottom of the screen read: Lee Jackson, chief of police, Fraser Winter Park Police Department. Closed captions scrolled across the bottom, tracking what the police chief was currently saying.

While fleeing last night, one of our fugitives, Cole Shipley, shot and killed one of our officers in an alley two blocks over my shoulder here. We are devastated. Deputy Tommy Johnson has been with our force for the past four years.

Jade's jaw dropped. Had she just read that right? Did it say her dad had shot and killed a police officer last night? She watched as a photo of Deputy Johnson in uniform appeared on the screen. The closed captioning said he had a wife and two young children. A bartender came over to ask Jade if she needed anything, but she was in too much shock to even acknowledge him, her eyes glued to the screen. The TV went back to the police chief behind the podium, who continued to speak.

Cole and Lisa Shipley have lived in our community for the past ten years. They have a fourteen-year-old daughter named Jade. We didn't know they were wanted fugitives on the run from the Feds for the past thirteen years until around nine o'clock last night when officially informed by the FBI.

Another photo appeared on the screen, this one of her parents when they were much younger. Her dad was heavier, with short hair and no beard. Her mom's hair was longer and blond. She'd never seen the photo before. An older newsreel began rolling. It was from a TV news station in Austin, Texas. A woman with a microphone stood outside a nice home with a lot of police activity going on behind her. A tag at the bottom said **Austin couple Greg and Amy Olsen suspected in murder of 21-year-old mother and kidnapping of her infant daughter.**

She gasped. Reading those words sent a shiver straight through her. Were her parents Greg and Amy Olsen? She'd never heard those names before. Was this real? Could her parents be murderers? Could she possibly be the baby they'd taken thirteen years ago in Texas? Was that why they refused to tell her the truth?

Jade felt her body trembling. She looked around, realized a couple of people sitting at the bar were staring over at her. This freaked her out even more. She spun, raced for the front door of the restaurant. When she hit the sidewalk, she froze again. She could see their van three rows back, sitting behind several other vehicles. Her mom was currently blocked from view by a big truck. Jade couldn't fathom climbing back inside right now. What was she going to say to her mom? Was she supposed to sit in the back of the van and simply cross over the border with two people who suddenly felt like dangerous strangers? She couldn't process any of this. It felt like a nightmarish out-of-body experience. She glanced over to her left at the shopping mall. She needed space to think about what she'd just discovered. She needed to be able to catch her breath and figure out what to do next. Her parents were going to be pissed, but she didn't even care right now.

Screw them. Screw the FBI. Screw everyone.

TWENTY-EIGHT

Lisa started to get concerned when ten minutes had passed and Jade had still not returned from the restaurant. What was she doing? Was she lying about trying to call Tyler? Could she have disobeyed again and borrowed a stranger's phone inside the restaurant? Annoyed, Lisa opened her door, stepped out into the drizzle, and hurried through the parking lot over to the front doors of the restaurant. She entered, looked around, but didn't spot her daughter anywhere. She walked through the main dining room and found the restrooms tucked away in the back corner. She stepped inside, but they looked unoccupied. She didn't see or hear anyone.

"Jade?" she said.

No response. She took a quick glance beneath two closed stall doors and didn't spot any shoes. She opened the first stall. Empty. Then the second. Also empty. What the hell? Where was Jade? Lisa left the restroom, crossed back through the dining room, and walked up to a young hostess near the front.

"Did you see a fourteen-year-old girl wearing a Taylor Swift sweatshirt come in here a few minutes ago?"

The hostess nodded. "Yes, she asked for the restroom. And then she stood over there in the bar for a few minutes watching the TVs.

She just ran out of here a minute ago like something was wrong. She looked really freaked out."

Lisa turned, stared over toward the bar area. Her eyes went straight to the middle TV, because she immediately spotted an older photo of her and Cole currently being shown on the screen. It was a picture from when they were back in Austin. Lisa felt her heart racing. *Oh no!* Had Jade just seen this? Was that why she had freaked out? She hurried over to the bar and moved as close as she could to the TV. A female reporter was holding a microphone, and it looked like she was standing on the sidewalk in front of a familiar Winter Park restaurant: Deno's Mountain Bistro. They dined there at least once a month. Lisa closely followed the closed captioning at the bottom of the screen.

Around nine thirty last night, here in Winter Park, police say a wanted fugitive named Cole Shipley shot and killed a police officer in this alley directly behind me. We're told Cole Shipley and his wife, Lisa, have been on the FBI's most wanted list after disappearing from Austin, Texas, more than thirteen years ago. Known then as Greg and Amy Olsen, they were suspected of murdering a twenty-one-year-old woman named Candace McGee and then kidnapping her baby. The woman had also been pregnant at the time. The case has been cold for years. But not anymore . . . Police and the FBI are still searching . . .

Lisa stared wide-eyed as more and more photos began popping up on the screen. Both from the present and the past. Jade was in several of them. Lisa thought about what the reporter had said about Cole shooting and killing a police officer. The FBI thought her husband had pulled the trigger? It ripped the breath out of her. He was innocent. Just like he'd been innocent back in Austin. How could this be happening again? Her mind returned to Jade. Had she just seen all this?

Lisa suddenly felt fully exposed. She was standing in the middle of a restaurant with dozens of people around, and her face matched the one being shown on the TV screen. Had anyone noticed her? She looked over to her left. A male bartender was staring right at her. His eyes bounced over to the TV, then back to her, and narrowed. Lisa swallowed, feeling even more panic shoot through her. She quickly turned around, kept a steady pace as to not look even more suspicious, and left the restaurant. Had the bartender put it together? Would he call the police? This was so bad. They needed to get away from here ASAP.

She hustled over to the van, praying the whole way that Jade had climbed back inside while she was in the restaurant. She slid open the back door. No Jade. Lisa cursed, feeling her world spiraling out of control. Where was her daughter? She spun around in the parking lot, looking everywhere. Her eyes settled on the mall. If her daughter had run, she had to have gone into the mall. That was the only thing that made any sense.

Lisa shut the van door, sprinted in that same direction.

She needed to find Jade, then her husband.

TWENTY-NINE

Burns understood why Chief Jackson in Winter Park finally chose to go forward with a press conference. After all, they had gone more than twelve hours without making an arrest, and the news had already started leaking out through social media channels. But he was still annoyed that Jackson hadn't sought his input before stepping in front of the TV cameras. If anything, it should've been a joint conference. This was an FBI investigation, after all. But Jackson was probably concerned Burns would try to steal the spotlight. He had to admit the old guy was indeed good in front of the cameras. The right blend of warmth, charisma, and authority. Burns hated standing in front of microphones. He thought he always sounded like a lifeless robot.

Burns and his team had just set up shop inside El Paso's FBI building when they got a call from local police that someone was claiming to have spotted one of their fugitives in a nearby restaurant. Burns thought that was probably too good to be true. With the press conference taking their investigation to the public, he knew they would likely start fielding a lot of random calls about their case. But they still scrambled to get into a black sedan and reached their destination across town ten minutes later. They parked in a large shopping mall lot in front of a Red Lobster restaurant. Six El Paso police vehicles were already on-site, red and blue lights flashing, cops everywhere.

"It's the van, boss," Davis said alertly, looking over to his left.

Burns perked up when he noticed two police vehicles parked directly behind a white van with GUNDERSON FAMILY PLUMBERS branded on the side. Three uniformed officers stood directly outside the van with their weapons drawn, ready for action. Burns spotted several more officers circling the exterior of the restaurant. This all looked very promising. Burns and Davis jumped out of the sedan and hurried over toward the van. He flashed his FBI badge at the first officer he encountered. The rain was coming down harder, and he could hear thunder cracking in the distance. He flipped up the collar on his dark-blue FBI jacket to try to keep the water from running down his neck.

"What do we got?" he asked, his eyes bouncing everywhere.

"Bartender called and claimed Lisa Shipley was in the restaurant. When we got here, we found this van that matches the description in your APB."

"Have you apprehended Lisa Shipley?"

He shook his head. "No, we're actively looking. Bartender said she left the restaurant right before he placed the call to us. The hostess said Lisa Shipley was looking for a fourteen-year-old girl who matched the photo of Jade Shipley. We've got everyone locked down inside that building. And we've begun to expand to the parking lot."

"What about Cole Shipley?"

"No reports on him yet."

"Anyone inside the van?"

"Not that we can tell. But we've been waiting on you to access it, as instructed."

"Good. Let's do it."

Burns and Davis quickly approached the van and pulled out their weapons. The two police officers who already had their weapons ready joined them. If Cole Shipley was inside, Burns knew they needed to be ready to defend themselves. Cole had already proved he was willing to kill to escape. But something told Burns no one was inside the vehicle. That would be too easy. And nothing had been easy in his pursuit of the

Shipleys. Davis put his right hand on the sliding back door and yanked it open. Everyone stiffened, ready to fire. But they saw no faces staring back at them. Davis poked his head fully inside, just to be sure.

"All clear," he said. "They're not here."

Burns holstered his weapon, stuck his head inside the back, and did a quick assessment. Two oversize pink beanbags, several blankets, a couple of large duffel bags, backpacks, a small cooler, and so forth. But no fugitives.

"You think they dumped the vehicle?" Davis asked.

"And leave all of this behind?"

"They could've panicked if Lisa thought the bartender recognized her."

Burns started unzipping bags. "No, they're still here somewhere."

"Why do you say that?"

Burns held up a small backpack and showed him the contents of the front pocket. It looked like thousands of dollars of cash. "Even when panicked, you grab this."

"Right. The mall?"

"Let's go find out before the police turn it into a three-ring circus."

THIRTY

Cole hurried out of the shopping mall, new burner phones he'd already programmed in hand, gray hood up over his head to block the sudden downpour. He was eager to get back to his family and get on the road. Being away from them for even twenty minutes without any way to communicate had left him feeling paranoid. He'd almost yelled at the store clerk, who was way too chitchatty, trying to get him to move along faster with his purchase. They were only a few miles from the nearest border crossing. Depending on wait time, he figured they should be inside Mexico and on their way to Sayulita within twenty-five minutes.

Cole rushed across the parking lot, head low to block the rain, but suddenly froze in place while looking up ahead. He cursed out loud, an exploding wave of fear sweeping over him. Police cars were everywhere around their van. Probably six or seven of them, with officers scrambling about all over the place. Cole quickly found the nearest vehicle in the lot and hid behind it for a moment. What the hell had happened? How had they found the van? Had Lisa and Jade already been arrested? He had to get closer to find out. He couldn't tell much from this distance. He moved out from the vehicle and navigated as hidden a path as possible with the other cars parked in the lot. He zigzagged back and forth, being super careful, until he found himself near enough to make out what was happening.

He didn't spot his girls standing out front anywhere. Cole scanned the police vehicles one at a time. He also didn't see anyone sitting in the back of any of the vehicles. That gave him some hope that Lisa and Jade had not been apprehended. Unless they were being held inside the restaurant. He doubted that. Cole took several breaths, trying to calm himself down and figure out what to do next. He regretted stopping to get the burner phones this side of the border. If his girls weren't out here, and they hadn't been arrested, where could they have gone? Turning around, Cole looked back at the mall. The only thing he could think of was that they'd gone to find him when the police somehow showed up. They were probably inside the mall right now searching for him. And if he didn't hurry and find them, the police would probably also be swarming the mall within minutes.

THIRTY-ONE

Brock sat with several border patrol agents at a hole-in-the-wall cantina near the Bridges of America border crossing in El Paso, buying everyone beer and appetizers, while also handing out copious amounts of cash—all part of his effort to recruit help at all three border crossings from El Paso into Mexico. He knew he needed an army out there if he had any chance of intercepting his targets before they got across. The cash rolls seemed to be working. Brock was promising a huge bonus to whoever discovered and held his targets until he got there. The young guys were burning up their phones recruiting help from all their work friends, acting like they'd all just won the lottery. Everyone could be bought. Even government officials. Especially on the border.

Brock quickly stepped out of the cantina when he got a text.

Police found the van!

He responded: Where?

Shopping mall called Cielo Vista. Get over there. Someone spotted the wife and daughter at a Red Lobster. No arrests yet.

On my way.

Brock slipped back inside to tell the border patrol guys to continue to recruit, tossed more cash on the table, then hurried over to a white GMC Yukon he'd rented at the airport. The engine rumbled loudly and he tore out of the parking lot. He was working the steering wheel and his phone at the same time, trying to pull up the exact location. The restaurant was only eight minutes away from him. He floored it. With each swift turn, the SUV's tires slid on the wet asphalt. He got to the shopping mall and circled through the various parking lots until he found the section with the Red Lobster. He stopped a good distance away, stared through the windshield as the wipers shifted back and forth to clear the raindrops. The police were everywhere. There was no way in hell he was going to be able to get close enough to handle any of this with a handgun.

Parking the Yukon, he reached into the back seat, grabbed his rifle bag, and pulled out his backcountry hunting rifle. He was probably going to have to do this from a distance. He just hoped he had enough time to get away after completing the assignment with so many cops around. He started devising his strategy. All he had to do was somehow get to the border. He'd just bought himself as much help as he needed to quickly get through and avoid being pursued. He would then camp in Juárez for a few days until everything died down again. It was a risky plan. But it was all he had. He couldn't blow this again.

After rolling down his passenger window, he positioned the rifle through the opening and put his eye to the scope. Now he had an up-close view of all the faces surrounding the restaurant and the van. He quickly searched the different clusters of people. So far, there was no sign of Cole and Lisa Shipley or their daughter. The police officers' body language told him no one had been arrested yet. But he could see a whole gang of officers searching the premises with their guns drawn. He knew the FBI was also on-site. They had all converged in one location, and something told Brock all hell was about to break loose.

He was ready for it. He thrived in chaos.

Pulling his eye away from the gun, Brock grabbed a small white cloth from his rifle bag to clean the moisture from his scope. The rain was really coming down now. While he did that, something caught his attention over to his right in the parking lot. He squinted. Someone was hiding behind a parked car and watching what was going on over at the police scene. Brock put his eye back to the scope and aimed his gun in that direction. He cursed. Cole Shipley. Before Brock could put his finger on the trigger, the guy was already on the move. He was darting in and out of vehicles, staying low, making his way back toward a mall entrance. Brock tried to line him up, but it was difficult. The guy kept weaving and bobbing. Brock knew he had only one chance to pull the trigger. He had no sound suppressor on his rifle. The shot would be loud and alert the cops. With one shot, they might not know where it came from. But multiple shots would put a direct target on him.

Brock steadied himself. Cole was now up on the sidewalk, ten feet away from the doors. It was now or never. Brock pulled the trigger. The bullet missed his target and shattered a glass door only inches behind Cole. He cursed. Setting the rifle down, he grabbed his handgun from the dashboard, jumped out, and raced toward the mall.

THIRTY-TWO

Jade maneuvered through the shopping mall until she found an Apple Store on the lower level. She told an eager store employee she was just looking around and then quickly settled herself on a stool over by one of the display laptops. After opening a web browser, she went to Google and typed in the names Greg and Amy Olsen. Her fingers were shaking so much it was hard to even hit the right letters on the keyboard. She scooted in close to the laptop to block anyone from peeking into her business. She held her breath as she watched the screen load with results. She again gasped out loud, drawing the attention of several other shoppers around her, but quickly played it off with a forced smile. Her eyes were locked on the screen. Every search hit was a news article about what had happened thirteen years earlier. All saying basically the same thing she'd just seen and heard on TV. Her parents had murdered a pregnant young woman and stolen her baby. She clicked through on one article and read more of the details. It said Greg and Amy Olsen had fostered to adopt nine-month-old Marcy McGee. There was a photo of her young parents holding the near toddler. Jade zoomed in as close as possible. She put her hand to her mouth. It was definitely her. She'd seen baby photos of herself in one of her mom's photo albums. She couldn't believe it.

She was Marcy McGee. Not Jade Shipley.

She kept reading. The Olsens had expected to be granted full custody of Marcy, but according to family accounts, they were devastated when the judge had switched course last minute and given the child back to her biological mother. The court had made arrangements for the Olsens to turn the child over to Candace McGee the next morning. However, police believed the Olsens somehow lured the young mother to their home that night and killed her with a kitchen knife. Police found the weapon at the scene of the crime. The Olsens then fled from the home with the child and were never seen again. She continued to search articles, reading the same thing over and over again, finding out that the FBI had immediately gotten involved and had been searching for them ever since.

Her eyes grew wet, and her hands were trembling. Her whole life was a lie? If they hadn't been caught, were they ever going to tell her the truth? Or would she have lived her entire life never knowing she'd been born a different person? How could her parents be so cruel? Did she even call them her "parents" anymore?

Tears now dripped on her cheeks. She couldn't stop them.

Her thoughts were interrupted by a familiar voice directly behind her. "None of it is true, Jade."

She spun around, saw her mom standing there. Jade didn't know what to say or do. For the first time in her life, she didn't want to reach for her mother when gripped with fear. It was an awful feeling. She just sat there, frozen.

Her mom stepped close to her, continued in a whisper: "I mean, it's true that we're not your biological parents. But we didn't kill your mother. We would've never done something like that. Something else happened that night, and it forced us to run away with you."

"What . . . happened?" Jade asked, her voice cracking. She felt a surge of anxiety hit her chest that made it nearly impossible to speak. This was her mom, but it wasn't her mom. That was impossible for her brain to handle right now. She desperately wanted to hear something that made sense. That made all this go away.

"Can we talk somewhere in private?"

Jade nodded. Her mom quickly led her out of the store and over to a Starbucks directly across the mall corridor. She asked her to have a seat at a small table away from everyone else. Jade's whole body continued to tremble. She felt so cold, and so alone. It was a feeling she'd never experienced in her whole life. Her parents had always been there. She'd always felt safe with them. But that had just been completely shattered.

Her mom spoke quietly. "I've thought about this moment for a long time. I've wanted to tell you the truth for years. I just never thought it would be under these circumstances."

"What is the truth?" she managed to ask.

Her mom swallowed. "You were our everything from the moment we began fostering you as a baby. We fell in love with you immediately. Your biological mother was in bad shape. Drugs, crime, jail, and other stuff. So we moved to adopt you. We thought you were going to be with us forever, and then the judge shockingly made a different decision. Yes, we were crushed. Beyond words. But we were never dangerous. Your mother came to our home in the middle of the night. She was bloody, panicked, and hard to understand. She begged us to take you and leave the house. She said you were in danger, and that someone was coming for you. And then she died right there in our entryway. We found out later she'd been stabbed. We were terrified. But to be safe, we left the house with you while trying to figure out what to do. We don't know exactly what happened next, but by the following morning, the police had made us the primary suspects in your mother's murder."

Jade's head spun. Was this really the truth? Could she trust what her mother was telling her? She'd never anticipated such a wild story. "If that's true, why didn't you just tell the police what really happened?"

"We wanted to but were afraid of what would happen to you. We knew child protective services would take you away from us. The chances of us ever being your real parents would likely vanish. We were terrified whoever did that to your mother would come back for you. And we wouldn't be there to protect you. The thought of putting you in potential danger was too much for us to bear. So we made the dev-astating decision to run."

"Then who really killed my mother?"

"We don't know. The police never focused their investigation on anyone but us. And although we tried, there was nothing we could do to change that narrative without potentially exposing ourselves. We never wanted to risk losing you. We felt we had no choice but to hide all these years."

Jade took a deep breath, trying to process all this new information. She was angry about being lied to her entire life. She felt a sudden lack of identity. Who was she anymore? But if what her mother was telling her was true, her parents had also sacrificed everything for her. Family, careers, home. There was no telling what else. They'd given up their whole lives to make sure she was safe and okay. She sighed, shook her head. She desperately wanted this to be true. Her mother had always been her best friend. She couldn't handle the thought of losing her. But she really didn't know what to feel right now.

"So how did the FBI find us?" she asked.

Her mom resisted answering her question.

"Tell me," Jade insisted.

"Your father had set up an offshore account under a different name and put a lot of money in it when we left Austin all those years ago. We never touched it. Until yesterday."

Jade's mouth dropped. "My surgery?"

Her mom nodded. "We think they must've been tracking it this whole time."

Jade cursed. Something she'd never done in front of her mom before. But she didn't care right now. "So this is all happening because of me and my stupid back?"

"No, Jade, it's happening because of all of us. We're a family."

Jade gritted her teeth. If it weren't for her back, none of this would've happened. Everything would still be normal. This wasn't fair. She wished she could go back and hide how much pain she was dealing with every day. Then maybe her dad wouldn't have touched the money. Jade suddenly thought about her dad, felt a catch in her throat. "But Mom, the news is saying Dad shot and killed a police officer last night."

"It's not true. Dad would never do something like that."

"Then why're they saying it?"

"We honestly don't know what's going on. Another man is involved. I'll tell you more, but we should get back to the van. Your dad is probably waiting on us and freaking out."

They stood, but Jade didn't move. She began to tear up again. Her emotions were running all over the place. She could barely control them. And while she was angry at her parents, the one thing she wanted more than anything right now was to be held by her mother. She desperately wanted to feel safe. And her mom had always been her safety net.

"What is it?" her mom asked.

"It's just . . . I love you, Mom."

Her mom embraced her.

"I love you, too. More than anything."

THIRTY-THREE

Cole fell flat on his face just inside the department store entrance. What the hell had just happened? He'd heard a loud boom in the parking lot, and then the glass door next to him had shattered. He pushed himself up, looked back. Was it lightning? That didn't make any sense. He would've felt the surge of electricity. Had the police just shot at him? Did they know he was running inside the mall? He stepped back toward the broken glass door and took a quick peek outside. His eyes first went to the police scene. It didn't look like anyone from that direction was headed his way. Then his eyes shifted left. And that's when he felt a punch to the gut. Across the parking lot, he spotted the stocky guy. He couldn't believe it. The guy was here in El Paso. And he was running through the parking lot, straight toward Cole. How was this possible? How had the guy been able to track them all the way here from Winter Park?

The answer didn't matter right now. Finding his girls and staying alive mattered. Cole spun around and took off running, threading through a group of shoppers who had come over to check out the ruckus around the glass doors. While he didn't want to cause a disturbance, Cole couldn't get himself to slow to a brisk walk. The panic wouldn't let him. So he just dismissed all the stares, shifted in and around the department store sections, and once again found himself entering the main mall corridor. He briefly stopped there to get his bearings. If his wife and daughter were inside the mall, where would they have gone? His only thought was they'd come inside to search for him. And if they knew he was looking to buy phones, they would've probably gone to the same upstairs electronics store he'd just left.

He took off down the corridor, this time trying to temper his speed; otherwise, all the stares would likely place a target on him. Would the stocky guy start shooting in the middle of a shopping mall? Cole didn't want to find out. He reached the escalator and began impatiently jostling his way around people on the way up. Reaching the top, he turned to look down behind him toward the entrance of Dillard's, searching for the stocky guy. There was no sign of him yet. But then he cursed. He spotted Lisa and Jade hurrying past the escalators back toward Dillard's. They were headed straight into the killer's path. He had to stop them. But he didn't want to yell out and draw attention to them. He jumped onto the descending escalator and began aggressively pushing his way down, repeatedly saying, "Excuse me, sorry," and drawing annoyed glares.

Reaching the lower level again, he hustled down the corridor after his girls. Cole grabbed both Lisa and Jade by the arms from behind, startling them.

"Cole?" Lisa said. "What're you—"

"This way!" he said. "Hurry!"

He yanked them both to the right.

"What is happening?" Lisa said. "We have to talk to you *right now*."

"Dad, stop!" Jade said, pulling back.

His wife and daughter tried to slow him down, but he resisted, nearly dragging them down a mall corridor over to the left. "I'm begging you. Run with me right now!" He locked eyes with Lisa. "He's here. The guy who killed the cop last night."

"At the mall?" Lisa asked, mouth dropping.

"Yes!" Cole's eyes moved past them, and he spotted the stocky guy finally entering the main corridor. This was so bad. He had to get them moving. "He's right over there!"

They began rushing down the corridor with him away from the stocky guy. But the guy already had eyes on them. Cole glanced back and spotted him running in their direction. They were now in a dead sprint. It no longer mattered that everyone was stopping to watch them. They had to get away. They circled around a children's play center directly in the middle of the corridor. Cole noticed a mall security cop standing up ahead and got an idea. He ran straight up to the mall cop, who seemed frazzled by the hysteria. Cole began pointing behind him and yelled as loud as he could, "He's got a gun! The guy back there has a gun!"

As expected, this immediately sent a ripple of panic through the entire shopping crowd. People began screaming and scrambling in all directions, trying to get away from whatever nightmare shooter situation they believed might be happening right now. Cole hoped either the security guard or the sudden chaos would somehow slow down their pursuer. They kept running down the corridor. The buzz of a shooter was rapidly expanding, and everyone in eyesight was now darting toward any exits or hiding spots they could find. They entered a huge Sears department store at the end of the mall corridor in a wave of other panicked shoppers. Cole took a right in the store, flying past perfume and jewelry counters, and stopped the three of them directly behind a clothing rack in the men's section.

He turned to Lisa and Jade. They were all panting. He handed Lisa one of the phones he'd just purchased. "Take Jade, get out of the mall, and run as far away as you can. Don't go back to the van. The police know we're here. Just keep running as far as possible and wait for me to call you."

"Dad, you have to come with us!" Jade insisted.

"I'll be right behind you. I promise."

It was a promise he was unsure he could keep.

"Cole, no!" Lisa added. "There has to be another way."

"There's not. Go! Please!"

They listened and continued to flee in the growing crowd of other runners. It was like watching dominoes fall as the madness picked up speed across the mall. But Cole couldn't go with them. He couldn't chance that the stocky guy might somehow catch up to them. The thought of a bullet piercing his wife or daughter was terrifying. If necessary, he would take the bullets for them. But that didn't mean he wanted to get caught. Stepping back into the aisle, he looked over toward the entrance to Sears, and waited to see if the stocky guy entered. He didn't have to wait long. The guy stormed inside, his head on a swivel, a gun clearly on display in his right hand. Cole didn't hide. He waited until the two of them locked eyes across the store. And then he took off running again. He zigzagged like crazy through the various clothing sections, tucking in behind every wall he could find, circling, ducking, and making his way to the back of the store completely opposite from the direction his girls had gone.

Cole entered an appliance section with refrigerators, washers and dryers, and dishwashers, and that's when he heard the first gunshot from behind him. It sounded the same as it had back in the alley last night. *Thump!* A store display right beside him exploded. Cole ducked even lower, darted behind another display, and then spotted a stockroom door behind the appliance section. He pushed through the swinging doors. He immediately entered a large warehouse section, with fork-lifts parked all about and several rows of two-story industrial shelving storing various heavy appliances. There weren't any employees around. They'd probably all bolted like the others. Cole shifted to his right, passed by several rows, trying to find a back exit out of the warehouse. He then noticed an open oversize garage door for loading and unloading at the end of the rows and took off toward it.

Reaching the garage opening, he momentarily paused to gauge the drop to the concrete below. Probably eight feet or so. He needed to be careful, as to not blow up his knee again. But he didn't get a chance to jump. He heard the double doors push open behind him. Cole froze, listened. When he didn't hear the casual movement of shoes on the concrete floor or hear anyone talking, he knew it had to be the stocky guy. He felt trapped. If he went for the jump now, he'd be a sitting duck. The guy would probably pick him off before he was even back on his feet again. He had to hide. And there was only one place to do it. He began quietly climbing up onto the sturdy warehouse shelf right beside him, reached the second level, and then squeezed in between several washer and dryer boxes. Peering through the boxes, Cole stared down at the open warehouse space in front of the garage door.

He heard the shuffling of shoes coming down the same aisle he'd just chosen. He tucked back a little, into the shadows, tried to measure his labored breathing. The stocky guy came into view directly below him, gun held out in both of his hands, and then peeked out the garage opening. Cole prayed the guy might assume he'd already jumped out and would choose to follow. But that unfortunately didn't happen. Instead, Cole heard the double doors to the warehouse push open once again. Whoever had just entered the warehouse also did so with measured steps. Cole carefully watched the stocky guy, who shifted away from the garage opening, then hid behind the aisle directly beneath him. If Cole sniffed right now, he was a dead man.

Then an unexpected voice boomed out from a couple of aisles over. "Cole Shipley? This is Special Agent Mark Burns with the FBI. I know you're in here. Come on out now so no one gets hurt."

Cole was shocked to hear Agent Burns. Was the FBI agent unaware the stocky guy had also entered the warehouse behind him? Cole wasn't sure what to think. On one hand, an FBI agent with a gun might save him from taking a bullet from a killer. But he also knew he would immediately feel the tight grip of handcuffs and most likely never see Lisa and Jade again. He didn't like either option, so he just remained completely still. So did the stocky guy standing below him, although he kept his gun ready. Cole heard Burns begin walking toward the garage opening. He was getting close to them.

"There's no use hiding, Cole. The police are everywhere. There's nowhere for you to go. So don't do anything stupid. Just calmly come out so we can talk. I've waited a long time to have this chat with you."

Cole saw Burns appear from the end of his aisle, gun in his hands, and step up to the open garage door. He was only ten feet away now. Cole peered straight down, swallowed. It looked like the stocky guy beneath him was getting ready to make his move on the FBI agent. The killer took a silent step forward. Then a second one. Then he raised his gun. The next step would be a kill shot. Cole felt dread stir up inside him. Was he really going to stay hidden and let the guy kill an FBI agent? That was unsettling. How much was he willing to sacrifice to get back to his family? The police officer getting killed last night in the alley was not his fault. He'd had no clue what was happening in that moment. But this would be real blood on his hands.

Cole felt his adrenaline racing. He couldn't allow that to happen. Even if he somehow got away and made it to Sayulita, he would never be emotionally free. He would live in a different kind of prison. He shifted slightly around the boxes to give himself more clearance to jump. When the stocky guy fully turned the corner and aimed his weapon at the back of Burns's head, Cole dived headfirst from the second level. His arm and shoulder landed square in the back of the killer's head, sending both of them straight into Burns. They collided like a three-car pileup: Cole into the stocky guy, the killer bashing into the FBI agent, and all three of them toppling hard to the floor. Cole heard metal clank on the concrete and figured someone had lost their weapon. Cole was up first, since he was the most prepared for the tumble. When the stocky guy tried to stand up right in front of him, Cole charged. He again put the full force of his shoulder into the man's chest—like a linebacker crushing a wide receiver—and sent him tumbling backward, straight out of the garage door opening, where the guy fell hard to the pavement eight feet below.

Cole didn't watch to see what happened next. He scrambled to his feet, spotted the garage door opener button on the wall, and began punching it as hard as he could with his palm. The oversize garage door quickly rumbled to a close. Looking down near his feet, Cole noticed a gun on the floor. He reached down, grabbed it, and came back up with it pointed directly at Burns, who had just found his footing again. It was clearly the FBI agent's gun, because Burns immediately lifted two empty hands in front of him.

"Take it easy, Cole," Burns pleaded.

"Don't move," Cole warned, his voice shaky, not even sure what to do next. He had to get out of there. But he had to somehow make sure Burns couldn't follow.

"What the hell just happened?" Burns asked.

"I saved your life."

"Okay. So who was that guy?"

"He's who you should've been searching for this whole time. He's the guy who shot and killed the police officer last night. And he's the man who I believe killed Candace McGee thirteen years ago, when she showed up on our doorstep already bleeding out. My lawyer sent you the video. But you did nothing. You've been wrong about all of it."

"Okay, put the gun down and let's discuss it."

"I wish I could. But like you said, the police are about to show up."

"You can't keep doing this, Cole. You can't keep running. We know you're attempting to cross the border to get to Sayulita right now. You can't hide from us in Mexico. You can't hide from us anywhere. So just put the gun down. And you can tell me all about how I've got this whole thing wrong. I'd love to hear it."

Cole was shocked to hear mention of Sayulita. How did he know? Where would they go now? There was no backup plan. He felt a measure of despair press in on him he hadn't felt in a long time. But there was no way he was going to put the gun down. Not with Lisa and Jade still out there on their own. Not with the stocky guy still a threat to all of them.

"Take off your jacket," Cole instructed.

Burns slowly took off his FBI jacket.

"Toss it here."

Burns did as told. Cole quickly slipped it on.

"Start walking," Cole said, gun aimed.

Cole quickly guided him over toward the front of the warehouse and began looking around at various tools and supplies stacked up on a small table against the wall. He spotted black duct tape and grabbed it.

"Turn around and put your hands behind your back," Cole ordered.

When Burns did, Cole pulled off the end of the duct tape with his teeth. While keeping the gun ready in one hand, he quickly wrapped the agent's wrists together like makeshift handcuffs. He then told Burns to sit down. Once the agent was sitting on the concrete floor, Cole wrapped his ankles so he couldn't stand. It was the best he could think of in the moment to immobilize the agent.

"Listen to me, Cole," Burns said. "This isn't smart. Think about Jade."

"Are you kidding me?" Cole hissed. The agent had no idea what he was saying. The sacrifices they'd made. The lengths they'd gone to. "Jade's all I'm thinking about. She's all I've ever thought about from the moment we left Austin."

"You keep running, she's going to get hurt. And that will be on you."

Cole's eyes narrowed. "You have a daughter, don't you? A teenager?"

The agent seemed surprised to hear that. "Yes. Why?"

"What would you do to protect her from danger?"

Burns took a moment, then said, "Whatever necessary."

"You're damn right."

Cole then put a final strip of duct tape over the man's mouth. Returning to the double doors, he peeked out and cursed. As expected, he spotted several police officers scrambling around the department store. Cole noticed someone's black ball cap sitting on a shelf right next to the double doors, grabbed it, and pulled it low on his forehead to hide his appearance as much as possible. He said a quick prayer and then stepped out into the chaos. He tried to move with a calm purpose, keeping his face as steady as possible, like he was an FBI agent on the job. He even held the gun out in front of him like an FBI agent would, although his fingers were clearly trembling. Two cops rushed straight toward him, their guns drawn, sending a chill up his spine. Would they immediately recognize him even while wearing the ball cap and the FBI jacket? Cole took a quick breath and willed himself not to panic. He spoke before they could speak to him. He was the FBI. He was in charge.

"Any sign of them?" Cole said, his brow stern, his voice firm.

"No, sir," answered one of the officers.

"What about you?" asked the other officer.

"Me neither. I've searched this entire side of the store. There's no one here. I don't think they came this way. We should head back inside the mall. Let's go!"

Both officers thankfully spun around and raced back toward the front of the store. But Cole didn't follow. He instead turned and rushed to another back exit from the department store. Before stepping outside, he dumped the FBI jacket and the gun into a trash can. He then pushed through the door and sprinted into the parking lot. The rain was coming down hard again. Small crowds of people had huddled in spots around various rows of cars. But thankfully no police. Cole quickly made his way into the crowds, just another shopper running for safety, but kept moving until he was clear of the mall property.

THIRTY-FOUR

Cole immediately called Lisa. They were safe and waiting for him more than ten blocks away. He caught up with them hiding in an alley between two old office buildings. He was completely drenched when he finally arrived—both from his own sweat and the steady downpouring of rain. His girls were sitting with their backs pressed up against a dingy metal dumpster and holding up a soaked cardboard box lid over them. For a moment, the dire reality of their situation hit him. Because they'd lost the van, they had no change of clothes, no dry shoes, no toiletries, no food, and no money—other than a couple hundred dollars in cash he still had in his front right pocket. They basically had nothing except the extra set of fake IDs he'd stuck in the back pocket of his jeans. However, they were alive and free. They would figure the rest out. They always did. His girls both jumped up and began hugging him.

"I'm so glad you're okay," Lisa said, burying her face in his chest.

"Me too," Jade said, hugging him from the side.

"I'm fine. I'm glad you're both okay, too."

It felt surreal that he'd survived the scary encounter in the department store warehouse. But he was still jittery. Especially after what Burns had told him about Sayulita. That was something they would have to talk about. They needed a new plan. He ushered them both back under the cardboard lid, to keep from getting further soaked, and they sat together on the wet pavement next to the dumpster.

"Dad, I know the truth now," Jade said.

Cole looked over at Lisa, surprised.

"I had to tell her," she explained. "She saw it on the TV. Our faces are once again all over national news right now. Our story is unfortunately being retold everywhere."

"I'm so sorry, Jade," he said. "We hated keeping this from you. Are you okay?"

"I honestly don't know how I feel right now."

Cole could see the turmoil in his daughter's eyes. It hurt. But she at least finally knew the truth. Hopefully they could rebuild from here. If they survived.

"I know it's hard to understand, but we did this for you," he told her. "I promise I'll do everything I can to regain your trust."

She nodded but didn't say anything.

Lisa spoke up. "Cole, how did that guy find us here? And why would he try to kill us even when there were so many police officers around?"

"I don't know. But I think we should try to go find those answers."

Lisa's brow furrowed. "What do you mean?"

"We can no longer go to Sayulita. The FBI is aware of it."

Lisa's eyes widened. "How do you know that?"

"I had a brief encounter with an FBI agent back there in the mall before I managed to get away. He told me this information to try to get me to surrender. But I'm not sure how they figured it out."

"Because I told Tyler on the phone," Jade admitted.

"What?" Cole said. "You swore you told me every detail of your phone conversation with him."

"I didn't want you to be even angrier with me. I guess we all lie sometimes to protect our own interests, don't we?"

Cole studied his daughter. Her face was firm. She was standing her ground. And he was in no position to chastise her at the moment. "Doesn't matter anymore. We can't keep running and hiding. I think we only have two options. Go to the FBI and put it all on the table. See if we can talk our way out of this mess by telling them everything we know. Hope for the best. Or we go back to Austin, where this all began, and see if we can figure out what really happened that night. If we can somehow solve that, maybe we can finally prove our innocence and get our real life back."

"How would we figure it out?" Lisa asked.

"Candace was clearly wrapped up in something that got her in serious trouble. Something sinister enough to get her killed. Before she died, she told me she was sorry. All these years, I thought she meant she was sorry about the custody battle. But now I wonder if she was apologizing for more than that. Maybe she was sorry for getting us involved with something more dangerous. Something big enough for them to still be coming after us all these years later. Like I said before, we're still a threat to them somehow. Maybe whoever is behind this is afraid Candace told us something that night that left them exposed. And as long as we're alive, we remain a threat. That's the only reason I can come up with as to why they would still be coming after us thirteen years later. Which means whoever is behind all of this is no small-time player. They have a lot to lose. And they are also powerful enough to somehow be tethered to the FBI, which I believe is how they found us in Winter Park yesterday, and in El Paso today."

Lisa's forehead bunched. "If they're connected to the FBI, we wouldn't be safe turning ourselves into the Feds."

"You're probably right."

"Then our only option is to go to Austin. Candace seemed to be close to her younger sister. She was always with her on her visitations, and her sister of course testified on her behalf. Do you remember her name?"

"Hailey McGee," he replied. "And she's exactly who I was thinking of going to first."

"You think she'd even talk to us?"

"We have to try. It's our only way forward."

"But how're we even going to get to Austin?" Jade asked. "We don't have a car anymore. Are we going to walk there?"

"I've already been thinking of a plan for that."

THIRTY-FIVE

Burns huddled with Davis inside the Cielo Vista shopping mall security office. They stood behind a mall security guard, who was currently at a desk working a keyboard. Several TV monitors situated in front of him showed security camera feeds placed throughout the mall. Twenty minutes had passed since a rookie cop had found Burns and finally cut him free from the stupid duct tape his fugitive had used to immobilize him. The whole thing had left him feeling humiliated. But he was also thankful to be alive. He'd never seen the unidentified man coming at him from behind with a gun. It had all happened in a flash. If not for Cole Shipley, Burns's daughter, Izzy, might be fatherless right now. But the whole thing had left him perplexed.

Outside of the security office, the entire mall was currently on lock-down. What felt like half of the El Paso police force had surrounded the property and were going store to store. It was a mess, but Burns appreciated the support. And yet there was still no accounting for their fugitives. If they got out, like he expected, Burns had absolutely no clue where they would go next. He felt certain he'd squashed their plans to head into Mexico. Cole would be an absolute fool to try that now. Just in case, they still had all border crossings covered. Desperate people sometimes do dumb things. But that wasn't the biggest thing occupying his mind at the moment. Who was the mystery guy with the gun? He'd had his team try to find the guy in the mall parking lot with no success.

"Right here," the security officer said.

He pointed at the middle TV screen. It was video from one of the main mall corridors from approximately thirty minutes ago. Burns could clearly see Cole, Lisa, and Jade Shipley running through the center of the mall. The security officer paused it on them.

"No, let it keep going," Burns instructed.

The guard pressed play again. Seconds later, Burns spotted the same guy who'd been inside the warehouse with him. Stocky, thick beard, blue jeans, cowboy boots, probably late thirties. He was running a hundred feet behind them. It looked like he already had a gun in his hand. Burns had been inside the mall when it all happened. He'd spotted Cole and his family from the upper level while looking down over the railing below. He'd pursued. But he'd never realized another individual was also involved until it was almost too late.

Burns leaned in and pointed. "Can you enhance it on this guy right here?"

The guard paused it, enlarged the image, and focused on the man in question.

Burns cursed. Cole hadn't been lying. It was indeed the same guy from the home security video taken thirteen years ago. What the hell?

"It's definitely him," Davis said. "He looks like a cowboy. But Myers still hasn't been able to ID him yet."

"Well, he wasn't helping Cole. At least, not this time around. Based off this mall footage, he was clearly hunting him down when I showed up."

"And Cole claimed this guy shot the police officer last night?"

"Yes."

"He offer any proof?"

"Didn't really have a chance to get into it. He had a gun in my face."

"Right. So what do you think?"

Burns frowned. "It's troubling. Who is this guy? And what's he doing here? Let's get this image over to our team and have them cross analyze any security camera footage we have from the sidewalks outside of the alley where the police officer was shot last night. See if this guy shows up anywhere."

THIRTY-SIX

Cole searched a mapping app on his new burner phone and found the nearest auto dealership to their alley was Casa Ford. With a crazy plan in mind, he left the girls behind and briskly made the fifteen-minute walk across a stretch of city. He kept the rain-soaked hood of his sweatshirt up over his head to hide his face the best he could. He didn't want to meet any wandering eyes out on the sidewalks right now. Thankfully, the skies began to clear, and the rain stopped.

When he arrived at the auto dealership property, he took off the wet sweatshirt and tossed it in the back of a Ford F-150 on the lot. His Denver Nuggets T-shirt was drier. He kept on the black ball cap. He was trying to look as normal as possible even though his blue jeans and running shoes were still drenched. Hopefully a salesperson wouldn't notice too much. He swiftly navigated through the many rows of cars until he got closer to the main building; then he perched himself in front of a new black Ford Explorer. He began circling it, looking in windows, knowing his presence would quickly draw a salesperson from inside the building.

It took barely sixty seconds before someone approached.

"Beautiful vehicle," said a voice from behind.

Cole turned around. He had no idea at this point if someone would recognize him from the news. When he saw stories like his own on TV, he rarely paid much attention to the actual faces of the people involved unless it was something happening locally. Both Winter Park and Austin were far away. But what he didn't know at this point was whether any local news had broken about them being in El Paso. It didn't matter. He had to risk it. They could do nothing without a vehicle. The sales guy was probably in his midtwenties, with a crew cut, wearing a blue polo and khakis, with a permanently wide smile. Cole locked eyes with him for a moment, holding his breath, waiting to see if there was any hint of recognition from the guy. The salesman just kept on smiling away, so Cole relaxed a little. So far, so good.

"Jonathan Pritchett," the sales guy said, sticking out a hand.

Cole shook it. "Dillon Foster."

"Great to meet you, Mr. Foster. You in the market for a new vehicle?"

"Yes, and I love this particular one." He put his hand against the Explorer. "Can I take it for a test spin?"

Cole wanted to get straight to it. He didn't have time for small talk.

"Of course!" Jonathan replied, the smile growing bigger. "Let's go grab the keys. I'll just need a driver's license and for you to sign a release form. Follow me."

Cole followed Jonathan into the main building, and his nerves grew more unstable. There were a lot of people meandering about and taking quick glimpses in his direction. Most were other salesmen, probably wondering if Jonathan had just gotten lucky with a walk-up. But Cole still felt uneasy about everyone looking over at him. He trailed Jonathan over to a small office. Cole could hear his wet shoes squeaking on the shiny tile floor with each step. It sounded obnoxiously loud to him. But no one else seemed to notice.

Right next to the office, Cole spotted a lounge area with several nice leather chairs and sofas facing a big flat-screen TV. His throat immediately tightened up. The TV was on a local news channel, and a photo of his bearded face was currently on the screen. His question about the news breaking that they were in El Paso had been answered. Six people sat in the lounge area watching. And a few salesmen stood around with their eyes also on the TV screen. Cole watched for a moment. Video footage ran from outside the mall, showing people running all about, and a male reporter was explaining the situation. Cole felt his body tighten up. If any of those in the lounge area glanced in his direction right now, they might easily put two and two together. It took a lot for Cole to not turn around and hightail it out of the dealership as fast as he could.

"Mr. Foster?"

Cole turned. Jonathan was waiting for him inside the office. Cole let out a quick breath, tried to calm himself, and stepped inside.

"Can I get you something to drink?" Jonathan offered.

"No, I'm good. But I'm kind of in a hurry, if you don't mind. Need to be somewhere in a few minutes to pick up the kids."

"Of course, no problem. Just need to borrow your driver's license."

Cole reached into his pocket, pulled out the fake driver's license for Dillon Foster. It was one of three options he had. The license was legit. If Jonathan ran it through a verification system, Cole felt sure he'd come out clean on the other side.

Jonathan gave it a quick glance. "Arizona?"

"Yes, we just moved here from Tucson."

"Cool! My uncle lives in Phoenix."

Cole didn't respond. Hopefully Jonathan would get the hint. No chitchat. The sales guy stuck the fake driver's license in a scanner and then handed it back to him. "Now just need you to sign this release form."

Cole reached down, wrote a fake local address and phone number, and then began to sign, before stopping himself midscribble. Out of habit, he'd started with a big cursive *C*. He quickly changed course, made it into a messy *D* for Dillon, and signed the document as Dillon Foster. He glanced up at the sales guy. Jonathan gave him a quick puzzled look. Cole silently cursed himself. What a stupid mistake. But he thought it best to not try to explain anything. That might only make it worse.

Jonathan stood. "All right, let me grab those keys, and I'll meet you at the vehicle."

Before stepping back outside, Cole watched the sales guy walk over to a big glass room where several men stood around a big counter with a huge row of file cabinets behind it. Probably the manager's office. He watched for a moment to see if Jonathan did anything more than just grab keys. Once inside, the sales guy spoke with an older gentleman. They both gave a glance through the glass in his direction. Cole felt like he suddenly had a big target on him. Had this been a huge mistake?

It was too late now. He was fully committed. But he was ready to flee at breakneck speed if he caught whiff of any potential threat. He stepped out of the building again, moved back over to the rows of cars. Another sales guy came over and offered to help. Cole told him he was already being assisted. But the more eyes put on him, the more uneasy he felt about all this. He was ready to get the hell out of there.

Jonathan finally reappeared. Cole couldn't tell if he had any keys on him. He decided if there were any further delays, he would bolt. He couldn't risk someone inside the building calling the cops on him right now. But thankfully Jonathan held out the keys.

"Here you go, Mr. Foster," he said, still showcasing his bright smile. "You want me to show you some of the bells and whistles?"

Cole took the keys. "When I get back. I want to see how it runs first."

"Yes, of course. If you want to get out on the highway and really open it up, the closest entrance is three blocks over from here. I think you'll be very impressed."

Cole quickly climbed into the vehicle, started it up.

Jonathan leaned into the door opening. "Take your time. Get a real feel for the vehicle. You can even go pick up your kids in it, if you want. I guarantee you and your family are going to love it. We can wrap this whole thing up today."

"Sounds like a plan."

It took all the restraint Cole had left to not kick Jonathan out of the way, slam the door shut, and then burn rubber out of the parking lot. He could feel his adrenaline racing. He was only seconds away from his plan working. By the time Jonathan realized Cole was never returning, they would be well on their way to Austin. And trying to track him down with the driver's license would prove useless.

Cole wondered how much time he would have before they called the police. An hour? Maybe two? Cole again thanked the sales guy, shut the door, calmly backed the vehicle out of the parking spot, and then eased through the lot. When he was completely out of sight of the dealership, he jumped all over the gas pedal.

Five minutes later, Lisa and Jade quickly climbed inside with him.

"I can't believe you really did it," Lisa said.

"I got lucky. Just hope the salesman doesn't get fired because of it."

"Well, we were due some good luck."

"We're going to make our own luck from here on out."

THIRTY-SEVEN

Burns was back inside El Paso's FBI building and set up in a small conference room with his team. Three hours had already passed since his encounter with Cole Shipley, and their fugitives were nowhere to be found. And neither was the mystery guy. Security footage from other retail strips around the mall perimeter was being analyzed. But it was needle-in-a-haystack stuff and would probably take them days to wade through it all. More than a thousand people had fled the property all at once. Burns still couldn't wrap his head around how everything had so bizarrely unfolded. If not for the unexpected appearance of the mystery cowboy, Burns felt certain they would have nabbed them at the mall.

But now he felt like they were starting all over again.

Agent Myers was situated at the end of a table, working his laptop, while coordinating with a team of other tech agents back in DC. Subway sandwich wrappers and empty Styrofoam coffee cups littered the tabletop. Burns was downing caffeine like it was the oxygen he needed to survive. Which felt like the truth right now, considering he'd gotten no sleep over the past thirty-six hours. Same with Davis. His right-hand man was running on fumes. Burns had already caught him nodding off several times while sitting in one of the conference chairs reviewing police reports on a digital tablet.

Burns rubbed his tight neck and continued to pace in a slow circle around the table. He wondered about Cole and Lisa's next move. He had to believe they were still hiding out in El Paso trying to figure that out. It was a huge city. Their van had been thoroughly searched. Based off everything they'd discovered inside—the duffel bags of clothes, blankets, toiletries, food, cash, and so on—Cole had been dead set on Mexico. That had clearly been the plan all along. But now what? Now where would they go?

"Sir, we got something!" Myers announced.

This stirred Davis awake. He bolted up out of his chair.

"Morning, sunshine," Burns said to him.

"Sorry, boss."

They both moved in behind Myers. Sidewalk security footage from Winter Park was currently on his laptop screen. The tech agent had been working tirelessly, analyzing footage from around the concert last night.

Myers said, "This was taken from directly across the street from the city park exactly six minutes before the police officer called in his report that he'd apprehended Cole Shipley in the alley next to Deno's Bistro." Myers pressed play. They watched as a group of people moved down the sidewalk toward the camera. Burns could see a massive crowd behind them over by the concert.

"Boom." Myers paused it. "Right there."

Burns leaned in, squinted, and cursed. Same guy. Beard. Jeans. Cowboy boots. It was plain as day. "I'll be damned. He was there."

"Yes, sir."

"Doesn't necessarily mean he shot the officer," Davis offered.

"Doesn't mean he didn't, either," Burns countered.

Davis tilted his head. "You starting to believe, boss?"

"I don't know what to believe anymore. None of it sits right with me. But I'll tell you one thing. I don't like that this guy appears in Winter Park right after we arrive there last night, and then he also shows up in El Paso today right after we get here."

Davis furrowed his brow. "You think someone on our end is giving out information?"

"Maybe. Start privately checking back channels. But try not to step into a hornet's nest. I don't need more problems to deal with back at the home office."

"I'm on it."

"Do the same with online channels," Burns told Myers.

"Yes, sir."

Burns's phone buzzed. He quickly answered it, listened for a minute.

"Are you kidding me?" he said into the phone, clearly exasperated. "Send me everything you've got ASAP."

He hung up and slapped his hand down hard on the table.

"What?" Davis said.

Burns looked up, shook his head. "That was El Paso PD. Cole Shipley stole a vehicle at a car dealership two hours ago."

"You can't be serious. How?"

"He walked right in with a fake ID. Asked to take a test spin in a new Ford Explorer. And then he drove off the lot and never came back."

"They're sure it was him?" Myers asked.

Burns looked down when his phone buzzed again. "He's texting me images right now."

He studied his phone and then held it up to show Davis and Myers. It was a security camera shot taken from inside the main building of the car dealership. Cole stood in the lobby wearing a baseball cap, T-shirt, jeans, and running shoes, looking like he didn't have a care in the world. Just a regular guy out car shopping.

"Meet Dillon Foster," Burns said.

Davis shook his head. "I'll give him credit. He's got serious balls."

"Sales guy said he encouraged Cole to take his time with the test drive, so he didn't think anything of it at first. After about an hour, he started to get concerned and called the phone number Cole had listed. Turned out to be an inoperable number. But the guy kept waiting, hoping it was just a mistake, and he could still get the sale."

"Two hours ago?" Davis asked.

"Yep. They could be anywhere by now."

THIRTY-EIGHT

They arrived in Austin around nine that night. The drive had been a full eight hours, even with minimal stops for gas and quick bathroom breaks. Texas was a massive state, and most of the journey was across wide-open West Texas plains. But Cole didn't mind it. It felt safer being out on country highways without much traffic around them. Cole and Lisa took it in shifts. He was exhausted and tried to sleep a little in the passenger seat while Lisa was behind the wheel. But it was difficult. Every time he closed his eyes, he relived his encounter with the stocky guy and the FBI agent. He kept wondering what had happened to the killer. The fall from the warehouse was around eight feet, and the guy had landed square on his side. The last thing Cole saw before shutting the garage door was the guy trying to roll over while grunting in pain. He could only hope he'd broken his collarbone or worse.

Much of the drive involved storytelling, as Jade now wanted to know every detail of their lives from the point when they left Austin thirteen years ago until the current day. With each passing hour, his daughter seemed to be slightly less abrasive and a little more accepting of her new reality. She got emotional when she found out she had real cousins, aunts and uncles, and even grandparents. Cole and Lisa had previously told her neither of them had siblings, her grandparents had all passed, and there were only distant relatives with whom they did not keep up. But they still couldn't promise her she'd ever meet them. Everything depended on what happened next when they arrived in Austin. They stopped at a Whataburger on the city's outskirts, and Cole quickly went inside and grabbed them some cheeseburgers. They ate in the car. They were almost completely out of money. They'd purchased some cheap dry clothes along the way at a Walmart. And they'd had to fill up with gas several times. Cole had no idea where they would sleep tonight. Could he even find a motel room somewhere for thirty-five bucks?

He decided not to focus on that right now and instead go over their game plan. Jade was already proving to be incredibly useful. She was more tech savvy than he was and had found a match for Hailey McGee, her biological mother's sister, on Instagram. Cole and Lisa were sure it was the same woman—she looked so much like her sister. From their online stalking, they figured out that Hailey was a single mother of an eight-year-old girl. And she regularly posted photos of herself working a waitress job at a place called the Hula Hut, which sat on the banks of the Colorado River near the edge of downtown—including one from an hour ago in which she posed with other waitresses. The tag read: Another night in restaurant paradise! LOL. The young women all wore khaki shorts and brightly colored tank tops.

"She's probably still there," Cole said. "If we hurry."

Lisa blew out forcefully. "But what are we going to do, Cole? Walk straight up to her in the restaurant and reintroduce ourselves? I'm sure news of the FBI finding us in Colorado has hit home here in Austin. Hailey has probably seen it and is reliving the nightmare all over again. She's not going to talk to us. She'll probably freak out and immediately call the police. I would in the same situation."

"Yeah, I know. I haven't figured that out yet. Maybe if we can get her alone—"

Jade interjected. "Or maybe I should be the one to talk to her first."

Cole's forehead bunched. "What? No way."

"Think about it, Dad," Jade continued. "If I go up to her and tell her who I am, I think she'd be shocked but also open to talking to me. I mean, I'm her sister's daughter. She's not going to call the police on her niece who's been missing all these years."

"I don't know," Lisa said. "Why would she even believe you're her niece?"

"I have a photo," Cole said, his memory jogged. "It's stored in a cloud album. I remember it clearly. I took it during one of the first visitations right after we started fostering you. Hailey was there with your mother, and she's holding you in her arms."

"I remember it, too," Lisa said.

"I could take your phone with me and show her the photo," Jade suggested. "Then I could try to convince her nothing was what it seemed with my mother's death. That the police got it all wrong. And beg her to come talk to you guys."

Cole hated the idea of sending his daughter alone into the fray. All he'd done for the past thirteen years was shield her from it. But he might have no choice.

"What if she doesn't believe her?" Lisa said, looking at him. "It could go badly."

Jade answered first. "Then I just get out of there and leave."

"I still don't like it," Lisa said, continuing to wrestle with the idea. "Anything could happen to you. And we wouldn't be there to prevent it."

"Mom, let me do this," Jade insisted. "Let me help *my* family."

Cole saw something in her eyes he'd never seen before. It was like she'd just grown up right in front of him. She was no longer his little girl. Jade didn't want to be protected by them anymore. She wanted to face her life on her own.

"She can do this, Lisa. Like you said, she's stronger than we think."

Lisa exhaled, finally nodded. "Okay. But be careful."

THIRTY-NINE

Burns and Myers sat down in a small conference room with a young guy named Jose Martinez at El Paso PD headquarters. Martinez had just started working as a border patrol agent three months prior. Eighteen, baby faced, and maybe 140 pounds, he claimed to have information relevant to their investigation. After quick introductions they got right to it.

"So what do you know?" Burns asked him.

"Yes, sir. This morning, a man was trying to recruit as many border agents as possible to help him look for certain people who may be trying to cross over into Mexico today. He was offering a thousand dollars up front to any agent who agreed to help and passing it out in cash rolls, so word spread quickly. Then the guy promised twenty thousand dollars to the agent who detained these people for him. We didn't believe him, at first, but then he showed us the cash in a black duffel bag. I didn't take it, but several guys did. I don't really blame them. We're all so underpaid. The guy texted a photo of who he was looking for. Later, I discovered it was the same people you've been searching for on your case."

"Cole and Lisa Shipley?" Burns asked.

"Yes, sir."

Martinez pulled up the photo on his phone and showed it to them. He said a friend had texted it to him. It was a family shot that had been all over the news today.

Davis quickly brought up his own photo of the mystery cowboy. "This the guy?"

Martinez studied the image, nodded. "Yeah, that's him."

"He give you a name?" Burns asked.

"No, sir. Just a phone number. Said to call with info. I have the number."

Burns turned to Davis. "Get that phone number over to Myers ASAP. Let's start tracking him down."

Davis hopped up and immediately jumped on his phone.

"Where did you meet him?" Burns asked Martinez.

"A cantina named Guerro's near the border crossing."

"Security cameras?"

"Not a chance. The place is a dump, sir. But great tacos."

"You see what this guy was driving?"

"No, sir. I'm sorry."

Burns thanked Martinez and asked him to stay in contact. This was a promising new lead. They desperately needed it. The afternoon had dragged on without any updates on their fugitives. While Burns doubted that they'd tried to cross into Mexico in their stolen vehicle—since the FBI had all three border crossings covered—he knew they could have already gone in a lot of directions by now. They might be all the way in California. Or Dallas. Or nearly to Las Vegas. Or they could still be hiding out around El Paso. The possibilities were endless. And that was maddening. Burns wondered if he'd officially lost them again. He remembered this same desperate feeling from many years ago. The thought of returning to his bosses empty-handed made him nauseous—especially after their investigation had hit national news again.

The day had not been entirely unproductive. Agent Myers had found three more security camera reels showing the mystery cowboy in Winter Park last night, including one of him walking out from behind a strip of buildings only three minutes after the police officer had chased Cole Shipley in the same direction. It was becoming more plausible by the moment that the guy could've been involved somehow with the shooting. But how and why?

Davis hung up the phone. "Myers says the phone is inactive."

"Damn. He probably dumped it after the mall incident."

"Most likely. Myers is going to keep trying."

"The guy sure was tossing around a lot of money."

"Twenty thousand dollars isn't chump change. Whoever he is, he has significant resources. Or works for someone who does. The guy is clearly a major player in all of this."

"The question I'm starting to ask myself is if he was a major player thirteen years ago, as Cole Shipley suggested, and I somehow botched it."

"If he was, *everyone* botched it. Not just you."

"Somehow that doesn't make me feel any better."

Burns's phone buzzed. Agent Myers. He quickly answered it on speaker.

"Sir, we got a hit on that secure website belonging to Cole Shipley. Someone just accessed the video file."

"You have a location?"

"Austin, Texas."

FORTY

Jade began a slow walk through a busy parking lot over to the Hula Hut, a Tex-Mex restaurant under a thatched-roof pier with lake views. Her parents had told her they would often come to the Hula Hut back when they lived in Austin, and had brought her as a baby many times. In the near distance over to her left, she could see the glimmering lights of the downtown Austin skyline. Jade had to admit she could feel her nerves jumping. She'd felt courageous when she'd insisted on doing this earlier. But as she stepped up to the restaurant's front doors, she started to doubt herself. What if Hailey McGee absolutely lost her mind when she identified herself? What if she screamed or passed out?

Jade knew she had to be ready for anything. Her mom had tried to role-play with her on the drive over—bringing up various possibilities—but there was just no way to know what she was in for without stepping inside the building. A small crowd hung around out front, probably waiting for tables. From the look of things, the restaurant was busy. That might not be a good thing if she was trying to get Hailey to stop and talk to her for a moment. She entered the building and was immediately met with the sweet smell of sizzling fajitas and the loud ruckus of a hundred people drinking cocktails and having a great time. Rather than roaming aimlessly, she threaded a group waiting in the small lobby and stepped up to a hostess who looked overwhelmed.

"How many?" the hostess said, barely even looking up.

"Is Hailey McGee working tonight?" she asked.

"Yeah, she's out on the back patio. You want to request a table out there?"

"No, I'm good. Thanks."

The hostess immediately went back to the mob. Jade shifted around the hostess stand and stepped into the restaurant proper. There was a bar on the upper level. The second level was a dining room. And through the downstairs windows, Jade could see multiple outdoor patio areas that sat right on top of the water. The phone in her hand buzzed. She held it up. It was a text from her nervous mom. **You okay?** She quickly clicked the like button, rolled her eyes, and moved down the stairs into the dining room. Her mom was probably going to text her every two minutes until she returned.

As she crossed through the tables, she had to be on her toes to not collide with waitstaff, who moved a mile a minute. Jade tried to imagine sitting in here with her parents as a baby. She obviously couldn't remember anything. But it made her mind wander. Her parents had another life. Under different names. In a different city. They were wealthy, lived in a big house, and drove nice cars. Which was so different from the life she knew growing up. She had a whole family she'd never met. Most were in Arizona. A family her parents hadn't seen in thirteen years. And she was about to meet her aunt. A woman who still thought her parents were murderers. It was surreal and still impossible to process.

"Excuse me, sweetie," said a waitress, flying through with a tray loaded with margaritas.

Jade quickly stepped out of the way, moved to the back of the restaurant, walked outside through a glass door, and entered the patio areas. There was another bar outside in front of her. And to her left looked to be an outdoor dining area. Jade scanned the bar first but didn't see anyone who looked like Hailey in there. So she walked to her left, climbed a short set of stairs, and then peered into the dining patio. That's when she found her. Jade swallowed the lump in her throat.

Hailey McGee. A wave of emotion immediately surged up inside and her eyes grew moist. She'd gone her whole life without having any extended family. And now she was suddenly standing in front of a woman who shared her same blood. Someone she didn't know even existed ten hours ago. Her hands were trembling. She wanted to bawl her eyes out right now but knew she couldn't. Not now. Later. Jade closed her eyes, took the deepest breath possible, and let it out slowly. Then she did it again. And a third time. She gradually started to calm herself down. After wiping her eyes dry, she looked at the phone and brought up the photo from more than thirteen years ago. Hailey held her in both arms, smiling up at the camera. According to Jade's parents, she'd been probably only seventeen or eighteen in the photo. That would put her in her early thirties now.

Hailey was thirty feet in front of her, circling an outdoor table, handing out meals. Jade could feel her heart begin racing faster as she approached. But Hailey didn't even look at her the first time she zoomed by. Her eyes were locked on a back door to the kitchen area. She pushed through the revolving door and disappeared. Jade chastised herself for letting her pass without a word. *Come on, be brave, you got this! You can't stand here all night!* She huddled out of the way in the corner of the patio until Hailey reappeared with another tray in her hands. Jade watched her distribute food to another table and once again head toward the kitchen.

One more quick breath. And then Jade stepped out in front of her, causing her to quickly stop to keep them from colliding.

"Sorry, honey," Hailey said.

"Hailey McGee?" Jade said, feeling her throat catch.

Hailey tilted her head. "Yes?"

"It's me," Jade said. "Marcy."

Saying that name out loud felt strange. Like she was talking about someone else.

For a moment, Hailey looked confused, her forehead wrinkling up. "Who?"

"Candace's daughter," Jade clarified.

She then brought up the phone to show the waitress the photograph. This made Hailey gasp, drop the empty tray, and put both hands to her mouth.

"Please don't freak out," Jade whispered. "I just need to talk to you."

Hailey's eyes were wide. "But . . . how? How're you here?"

"Can we talk in private? Please."

For a few seconds, Hailey didn't even move, her eyes locked on Jade.

"You all right, girl?" asked another waitress, who was exiting the kitchen.

Hailey seemed to realize she was just standing there, blocking everyone.

"Yes . . . yes, I'm okay," she stammered, but her eyes never left Jade.

"Please," Jade said again. "It's really important."

"This way," Hailey said. She moved down the steps, circled around the outdoor bar, and led Jade over to a pier with several boats tied up. She didn't look all that happy when she turned back around to face Jade again. "Is this some kind of cruel joke? Did my ex put you up to this because of the news right now? Joel is so damn mean."

"I don't know any Joel," Jade said. "But it's really me. I promise."

Hailey again put her hands to her mouth. "You do look so much like my sister." Then her eyes grew wet. She reached out with both hands, immediately grabbed Jade, and pulled her in for a hug. It felt weird to hug a stranger, but Jade didn't fight it.

"I can't believe this," Hailey said, stepping back, tears rolling down her face. "But how're you standing here right now? I've been watching the news. I saw where you'd been found with those horrible people in Colorado."

"Because those people are here with me."

Hailey's mouth dropped. "What?"

Jade spoke quickly so Hailey wouldn't panic. "They're not horrible people. They did not kill my mother—your sister. Someone else did that night. And they only took me to keep me safe from the same dangerous people."

Hailey frowned. "They've brainwashed you."

"No, I promise you that's not true. Someone has been trying to kill us while we've been running from the FBI the past two days. That's why we're back here in Austin. I need you to talk to them. Because we believe it's the same person who killed my mother. And if we don't figure it out, he could kill me next."

Hailey's eyes narrowed. "Do you know how crazy this all sounds? I should . . . I should probably call the cops or something."

"No, please don't. If you ever cared about me, you won't do that."

Hailey swallowed, her eyes growing wet again. "I did care about you. So much. I was heartbroken when they took you. I just . . . I can't believe this. Look at you. You're beautiful."

"Well, I have a chance to be back in your life now. If you'll help us."

Hailey took a deep breath, let it out slowly. "Where are they?"

"In the parking lot up the hill."

She glanced up the hill, bit her bottom lip. "Okay, give me a sec. Let me get someone to cover for me."

FORTY-ONE

Cole had parked the Ford Explorer in the very back of the lot, where they could easily see everyone who approached from the restaurant down the hill. Lisa was sitting in the passenger seat. He held her hand, trying to keep her calm. It didn't seem to be working. With each passing second without seeing their daughter return, Lisa gripped his hand tighter. It felt like she was cutting off the blood circulation.

"Should I text her again?" Lisa said.

"No, give her more time."

Lisa huffed. "It's been too long already. We should've never allowed her to do this."

"It's only been fifteen minutes, Lisa. Be patient."

She looked over and frowned hard at him. "It's impossible to be patient when our whole world is down there by herself somewhere. The police could literally be coming at any moment and taking her away from us. If that happens, I'll never forgive myself. I'll fall completely apart. They might as well lock me away in the psych ward."

"No one is locking you away. Because here she comes."

They both perked up, stared through the windshield. Jade appeared first and was then followed closely behind by Hailey McGee. No one else was with them.

"She did it," Cole said.

"Thank you, Lord," Lisa whispered.

They both got out of the vehicle, circled around to the front, and stood there waiting. They wanted to look as disarming as possible. Jade kept walking toward them, but Hailey paused about ten feet away. She stared at them both for a good long moment. Her face grew pale, as if she were looking at ghosts. Lisa quickly pulled Jade into her safe arms, hugging her tightly. Jade handed him back his phone. He took a step toward Hailey.

"Thank you for coming," Cole said in his warmest voice. "I'm sure this is weird, and probably a little scary."

"*Horrifying* is more like it," Hailey replied. "The two of you have been the focal point of my nightmares for years."

"I'm sorry," Cole said. "I'm not sure what all Jade told you—"

Hailey interrupted. "She says you didn't do it. It was someone else."

"She's telling the truth. And we need your help to figure out who and why. I have a video of the man we believe was involved in Candace's death. Can I show it to you?"

Hailey looked uneasy but shrugged and nodded. He cautiously stepped over to her as to not spook her. A few feet away, he brought up the video of the stocky guy he'd taken from their home security camera the night of her sister's death. He'd pulled it off his secure website just moments ago. He paused the video with a direct view of the guy's face.

"Do you recognize him?" he asked.

Hailey squinted. For a second, she didn't say anything. She just kept staring. "Where was this taken?"

"It's from our home security camera thirteen years ago. Candace showed up to our house first. She was bleeding and panicked. When I let her inside, she fell right into me before hitting the floor. She said someone was coming to harm Jade—or Marcy—and then she begged us to leave right away. To take her and protect her. She died before I could even call for help. The guy in this video showed up moments after we left the house."

Hailey looked at him. "But the police said they found the murder weapon. One of your kitchen knives. With your fingerprints on it."

"We think the guy in the video used one of our knives posthumously. To lead the police in that direction. That's why my fingerprints are on it. And then he deleted all the security camera footage. We were fortunate to save this video before that happened."

"Oh my . . ." Hailey covered her mouth like she might be sick.

"I'm sorry to be so graphic. I know how awful this must be for you."

"But why didn't you just tell the police the truth?"

"We tried. We sent the video I just showed you to our lawyer to share with the FBI. But it didn't make any difference. So we kept running. We knew they'd take Marcy from us. And if they did, that would just put her right back in danger. Your sister clearly believed whoever did this would have no issue harming a child. We were never going to allow that to happen. But we almost did today. The same guy in the video tried to shoot and kill us earlier this afternoon."

"This is crazy," Hailey said. "I do recognize him."

"You do?" Lisa said, stepping forward, immediately engaged.

Hailey nodded. "But it was way before the night of my sister's death. Probably a year and a half or so. I remember meeting him at a bar. Candace dragged me there. Some sharp-dressed business guy in a suit was all over her that night. He was probably twice her age. But my sister never cared about that. She could tell he had money, so she was interested in him. We were so damn poor. My dad left us when we were little, and my mom was an alcoholic. Still is. Candace and I only had each other growing up. Anyway, the guy in your photograph was with the man in the business suit. I hung out with him while my sister and the other man sat there groping each other."

"Do you remember his name?" Cole asked.

She shook her head. "It was just one night."

"What about the name of the guy in the suit?" Lisa asked.

Another headshake. "I mean, this was so long ago. But I do remember the two guys had an odd relationship. It wasn't like they were normal drinking buddies. It was more like the guy in the photograph was also the other man's security or something. When I asked him to play pool, he declined and said something about him needing to be within eyesight of the other man. So I figured the guy in the suit must be someone important."

"But you didn't recognize the man in the suit from anywhere?" Cole said.

"No," Hailey said, running a hand through her hair. "I don't understand. How could the guy I met that night in the bar be involved with my sister's murder?"

"That's what we're trying to figure out," Lisa explained. "Do you remember anything else about the guy in the photo?"

"Yeah, I mean, he was real cowboy-like. He wore boots and Wrangler jeans. And he talked with a West Texas twang. A little too much for my taste. He was hitting on me and trying to impress me. I think he told me he managed some big ranch. He really bragged about it, saying something about it being one of the biggest ranches in Texas. I remember he even had a tattoo of the ranch's brand."

"On top of his hand?" Cole asked.

She thought about it for a second. "Yeah, his right hand."

Cole made a mental note to look up ranches and see if it led anywhere.

"I don't remember much else," Hailey said. "I got bored and left early."

"You ever see either of the guys again?"

"Nope."

"What about your sister?"

"Not that she ever told me about."

"You mentioned this happened way before the night your sister died," Lisa said. "Do you remember a more specific timeframe?"

Hailey kind of laughed. "Funny. I remember the exact day. Sort of. It was the day Texas beat Texas Tech fifty-six to zero. I remember because my boyfriend at the time was a huge Red Raider fan. He had family out in Lubbock. And he was so pissed off that night after the game. I couldn't even be around him. That's how I ended up at the bar alone with my sister." Hailey sighed, shook her head. "I can't believe this is all true about Candace."

"I'm sorry," Lisa said. "I'm sure this is like ripping the Band-Aid off all over again."

"No, it's okay. I just . . . I'm just so shocked to be standing here looking at Marcy, almost all grown up. I know that day in court was horrible for you guys. But my sister really did want to be a good mother. She worked hard to pull herself together. She was excited about the future. She told me she had a plan to finally get us out of poverty. That we weren't going to have to fight and claw our way through life anymore. She said she was going to take care of us."

"What kind of plan?" Cole asked, eyes narrowed.

Hailey shrugged. "I think it had something to do with the tech world, because she told me one of her old high school nerd friends was helping her. I figured she might be doing some kind of nudie website or something to make money. We knew a girl from high school who was making a fortune doing that kind of thing."

Cole wondered if it could be something else entirely. "Do you still keep in touch with this high school nerd friend who was helping her?"

"Here and there. He's a tattoo artist at a place called BlindSide on Sixth Street."

FORTY-TWO

After thanking Hailey McGee, Cole promised they'd be in touch as soon as they could. And then they quickly drove away from the Hula Hut, parked in the back of a grocery store parking lot nearby, and sat there together trying to figure out what to do next. While Cole searched up brand logos for the biggest ranches in Texas on his phone, Lisa and Jade began scouring old football schedules, looking for the exact date the Longhorns had shut out the Red Raiders many years ago. Cole started with a top-ten list for ranches. From there, it was easy for him to find a match. The brand was for Longshore Ranch, the third biggest in Texas, at more than half a million acres. The symbol was a convoluted *L* twisted with an *R*. It was difficult to decipher upon casual glance. But it was clearly the same as the tattoo on the guy's hand.

Cole could feel his adrenaline start to race.

They were getting a little closer to the truth.

He continued to read up on the massive ranch. It had belonged to the powerful Nelson family for more than a hundred years. Based on his research, the family was unimaginably wealthy and had been influential political players for decades. At seventy-nine years old, Edward Nelson was the current patriarch, having taken over from his father nearly forty years ago. It was easy to find photos of past presidents standing with him while visiting the ranch throughout the years. The patriarch had three sons. The oldest helped run the family empire. The second was a prominent surgeon in Houston. The youngest had become a lawyer. And then he had parlayed his legal career into becoming a Texas Supreme Court Justice more than a decade ago. But it was what Cole realized next that shook him and caused him to curse out loud.

Lisa looked up. "What is it?"

"I found where the stocky guy in the photo works. It's called Longshore Ranch. Third biggest in Texas. A super-wealthy family has owned it for the past century. The youngest son, Peter Nelson, is currently the presidential nominee to become the next United States Supreme Court Justice."

Lisa's mouth dropped. Cole didn't pay much attention to politics or the happenings in DC, but he knew all about the confirmation hearings this past week. It was the biggest news story going on in the country right now. The thought that they could be directly or indirectly connected to it was both shocking and scary as hell. They sat in silence for a moment. It was like a bomb had gone off in the car, and they were all just sitting there trying to recover from the explosion.

Jade finally broke the silence. "What does this mean, Dad?"

Cole swallowed, exhaled. "It means the guy who tried to kill us today and who likely killed your mother thirteen years ago works for the same family whose son is only days away from becoming one of the most powerful people in the United States."

"This is crazy," Lisa said, trying to digest the information. "Do you think there is any chance what is happening to us right now could be connected to that?"

"It's possible. Have you found the date of the football game yet?"

"Yes," Jade said. She'd commandeered her mom's phone. "Texas beat Texas Tech fifty-six to nothing at home on Saturday, November 2, fifteen years ago this fall."

Cole pulled up a career timeline for Peter Nelson. "Judge Nelson was a partner at a law firm in Austin when that game occurred. He would go on to be elected as a Texas Supreme Court Justice the following year."

"You think he could've been the sharp-dressed businessman who Hailey saw in the bar with Candace that night?" Lisa asked.

"It's possible."

Cole did quick math in his head. He again let a curse word slip out.

"What, Dad?" Jade asked. "What is it?"

"That night in the bar was almost exactly nine months before you were born."

Another bomb dropped. They all just stared at each other a moment. It felt like things were escalating by the second right now. They'd discussed with Jade earlier during the car ride from El Paso how her father's identity had never been part of the legal proceedings when they were fostering to adopt her—Candace had kept it out of play, claiming in court she wasn't sure who the father was. But was that a lie?

"You think he could be my biological father?" Jade asked.

"I don't know, Jade," Cole said, his mind churning. "But what if Candace's so-called plan was not putting together some kind of sexy website, like Hailey suspected? Peter Nelson would've been in the middle of his first campaign for the Texas Supreme Court when Candace was killed. What if her plan to finally get them out of poverty involved blackmail?"

Lisa's eyes widened. "And he sent someone to kill her?"

"I know it sounds crazy. But history has proved that powerful families will often go to great lengths to protect their power."

FORTY-THREE

The chartered FBI plane was beginning its descent into Austin and would touch down shortly. Burns had tried to sleep a little, but he kept replaying today's events in his head. Why had Cole Shipley risked his life to save him? A man guilty of murder doesn't usually do that. Burns knew that once a criminal opened that violent door, they were much more prone to continue operating within that violence. But Cole had detoured from that path by preventing a new death—even in his most desperate moment. Why? Could what the man was claiming happened in Austin all those years ago actually be true?

Burns was staring out the small window into the darkness of night when Myers suddenly scooted over to him with his laptop.

"Sir, El Paso PD discovered a vehicle in the mall parking lot that had a window rolled down and a hunting rifle sitting in the front passenger seat. They think it's the weapon that was used when the glass door at the entrance of the mall exploded."

"They run the plates?"

"Yes, sir. It's a rental car from Avis. Rented that morning at the airport by a man named Brock Gunner. I just ran a simple Google search on the name."

He turned his laptop screen toward Burns, who squinted. It was a color photo attached to a news article about local rodeo results from the *Lubbock Avalanche-Journal*. The article was dated around eight years ago. A stocky guy probably in his early thirties, wearing a cowboy hat, boots, and dirty jeans, stood among a group of other cowboys and held up a huge Western belt buckle—an award for his bull riding. It was clear as day it was the same man who'd tried to kill Burns back in the Sears warehouse, if not for the intervention of his fugitive. The same man from the video taken thirteen years ago at Cole Shipley's house.

"I'll be damned," Burns said. "We got him."

Burns turned and looked across the aisle, where Davis was sleeping and snoring with his mouth wide open. Burns grabbed an empty water bottle and tossed it in his direction. It hit Davis in the head and startled him awake. He jolted upright, looking confused, trying to figure out what had just happened.

"Get over here," Burns said. "We found our mystery cowboy."

Davis stretched his neck. "Didn't even realize I'd fallen asleep."

"You've been snoring like a freight train the whole flight."

"Sorry about that." Davis slipped out of his chair and leaned in behind Burns to have a good view of things. "Brock Gunner. That's definitely him."

"What do we know about him?" Burns asked Myers.

"Not much yet. I just started digging. His driver's license is registered in Lubbock. Looks like he works at a huge ranch called Longshore. It's owned by the Nelson family."

This caught Burns's attention. "The Nelson family as in Peter Nelson?"

"Yes, sir."

Davis spoke up. "We're talking about the Supreme Court candidate?"

"Correct," Myers said. "The same family."

They all sat there in silence for a moment.

"Could be completely unrelated," Burns finally said.

"Right," Davis agreed. "But then why is some cowboy from Lubbock chasing our fugitives across the country?"

Myers added, "And what was he doing in Austin at the Shipleys' house the night they disappeared?"

Burns studied Brock Gunner's face on the laptop.

"That's what we need to figure out. And fast."

FORTY-FOUR

The family's private plane touched down in Austin. Brock quickly climbed down the stairs and hobbled over to a Dodge Ram truck, where one of his former ranch hands was waiting behind the wheel. Brock thought he might have broken a bone or something in his ankle in the fall from the warehouse back in El Paso. He had for sure separated his shoulder. Both hurt like hell right now. But he couldn't do a damn thing about it until he finally ended this whole thing. He'd taken a handful of Advil on the plane and chased it down with a glass of bourbon, trying to carefully walk the line between numbing the pain while still functioning at a high level. But he was buzzing a little more than he wanted right now.

"You look like hell, Brock," said the driver.

"You're going to look the same if you don't get this damn truck moving."

The guy grinned and stomped on the gas, and they began to exit the airport property. Brock pulled out his phone and made a call to the driver's brother, Judd. Both guys used to work for him on the ranch but had moved to Austin a couple of years ago to pursue rodeo full-time.

"Yeah, I'm here," Judd answered.

"You still on them?" Brock asked.

"Yep. They just parked a block off Sixth Street."

"Don't let them out of your sight, Judd. I'll be there shortly."

"You got it."

Brock hung up. When he'd been informed earlier that Cole and Lisa Shipley had come back to Austin, he had speculated a few possible reasons: One, they had stored money somewhere and needed to return to get it. Two, they wanted to see family before he or the FBI caught up with them. Or three—and this was the most dangerous—they were going to try to figure out who'd really killed Candace McGee thirteen years ago and see if they could somehow exonerate themselves.

Brock obviously couldn't allow that to happen. He'd immediately recruited help around town. Several guys in the capital city owed the family favors, and he was calling them all in right now. He'd sent them out to monitor various people around town he suspected Cole might try to find. Brock had a short list of people who had been closely associated with Candace McGee years ago, and whom they'd monitored for a brief time in the aftermath of the woman's death. Just to make sure none of them knew more than they should or caused any trouble. No one did. One person on the list was Candace McGee's sister, Hailey. She had been easy to find. They'd struck gold by trailing her only minutes ago. Judd had followed the Shipleys from the Tex-Mex restaurant.

The guys out there helping him were to follow and nothing else. They weren't killers. That was his job.

Brock made another quick call. It was immediately answered.

"You better have good news for me."

"We have eyes on them. I'm headed to them right now."

"Good. Finish this tonight, Brock. I can't sit in front of a national audience tomorrow with this damn thing hanging out there and dominating my mind."

FORTY-FIVE

Cole parked a block off Sixth Street, Austin's famous bar and entertainment district. The plan was for him to go alone to try to find and talk to the tattoo artist. There was no reason for all three of them to expose themselves out on the sidewalks of Austin. Especially in a wild place like Sixth Street, where there was a heavy police presence. As soon as he got out of the vehicle, Cole could hear live music booming out of a host of venues. Jazz. Pop. Rap. Country. Classic Rock. It could all be found on Sixth Street. He hadn't been there in more than fifteen years, but it looked like nothing had really changed. Many of the same bars were still going strong. The entire street was still blocked off at night and the crowds of people were still packed in tight. It was Sunday night and the last chance for Austin's party crowd to get their groove on before college classes and the professional workweek took back over.

Cole put on a pair of nearly transparent sunglasses he'd purchased at a gas station and kept the hood of his new black sweatshirt up over his head. He wasn't going to take any chances on being recognized. Thankfully, people wore all kinds of weird clothes, glasses, and hats on this street. He peeked at the mapping app on his phone. BlindSide Tattoo & Piercing was a block up ahead of him on his left. He began quickly threading through the dense crowd. As expected, the police were everywhere. Arrests were made every night on Sixth. Cole already spotted two uniformed officers sitting up on police horses. He could see the same kind of grouping only a block away. He made sure to stay as far away from them as possible.

He spotted Voodoo Doughnut up ahead and knew the tattoo parlor was directly across the street. More weaving in and out of the crowd, passing by Darwin's Pub and the Soho Lounge, before finally stepping up to the bright-blue and black front of BlindSide Tattoo & Piercing. The lettering on the outside of the glass door said the shop was open until two thirty every morning of the week. He opened the door, moved inside, and climbed a set of stairs. BlindSide was on the second level. He entered a cool and spacious lobby with black leather sofas, chairs, mirrors, hardwood floors. Most of the seating was currently occupied. The place was busy. Heavy metal music was pumping.

Cole approached a glass counter, where a young woman with pink hair, several nose piercings, and full sets of tattoos covering both of her arms looked up at him.

"Hey," she said. "What can we do for you?"

"Is Jack Harlen working tonight?"

"You bet. Every night. You got an appointment?"

"No, I'm a walk-in."

"Can I get your name?"

"Seth Rutter."

"You done this before?"

"Get a tattoo? No, first time."

There was no reason to lie. His eyes scanned the room, looking for the guy they'd already identified from looking up his Instagram account.

"Well, Jack's currently finishing up a job. But Cliff is open right now, if you want to get started right away."

"No, it really needs to be Jack. My friend says he's the man."

She smiled. "He is the man. He did this whole arm."

She held up her left arm, twisted it to show him all angles. It looked like a fiery Dungeons & Dragons scene.

"It's beautiful," he said, engaging the best he could.

"Thanks. All right, let me go see how much time he has left. Be right back."

"Okay, thanks."

The young woman slipped away from the counter and followed a hallway. Cole exhaled and his shoulders dropped a bit. He really hadn't wanted to have to try to track down Candace's old high school friend if he wasn't at the tattoo parlor tonight. He pulled his phone out, quickly typed a text message to Lisa: He's here. About to speak with him. She immediately hearted his message. He sent another text: You guys okay? She responded: Yes. No issues. Just anxious. He hearted her message. Cole then spotted the tattooed girl returning from the back hallway.

"Jack is actually about to wrap up," she said. "So you won't have to wait too long."

"Great."

"Can I get you something to drink? Whiskey? Tequila? Believe me, a shot of either can really help first-timers like you."

He grinned. "I bet. But I should be good."

"All right, I'll take a shot for you. Have a seat. He'll be right out."

FORTY-SIX

Lisa reclined low in the passenger seat. Jade was in the back. They'd all bought new hoodies at Walmart on the way to Austin and both currently had their hoods up. Although they were a full block off Sixth Street, there was still quite a bit of streetlight and busy foot traffic on the sidewalk next to them. Most walkers paid little attention to them sitting in their vehicle. A few did, and it made her nervous. She was starting to wish they'd parked farther away. But Cole wanted the vehicle close by in case they needed to make a quick getaway for some reason. Lisa was about to text her husband again, to get a status update, when she suddenly spotted bright headlights move in directly behind them. When red and blue flashing lights suddenly went off, Lisa felt her heart nearly stop.

"Mom!" Jade shrieked from the back. "The police!"

"I know, I see them. Just stay calm."

"Why are they behind us?"

"I don't know. Just don't panic."

Lisa said this even though she was freaking out internally. Why was a police officer back there? Had they already been found again? There was no time for them to get out and walk away from the vehicle as a precaution. Lisa was cursing and praying at the same time. A uniformed officer was already out and moving up the sidewalk toward the driver-side window. He looked to be in his early thirties and very clean-cut. He leaned into the vehicle and tapped on the glass. Lisa let out a deep breath, tried to steady herself. She put her shaky hand on the door lever and lowered the window. Her heart was in her throat.

"Ma'am, are you aware you're illegally parked in a loading zone?" he said.

She was grateful to hear that. He was at least not initially arresting them.

"No, officer. My husband parked here. He must not have seen the sign."

"Where is your husband?"

"He'll be back soon. He's just dropping something off."

"Can I see your license and registration?"

Lisa swallowed again. "I don't have that with me. But I can move the vehicle, if you want. This was an honest mistake."

"Just wait here. I'll be back in a moment."

He walked back over to his vehicle and climbed inside. Lisa's heart was pumping so hard she could feel it in her head. Was the cop about to run their plates? If he did, would it show up as a stolen vehicle? She had to suspect it would. Had the police in El Paso already put together that the thief was a fugitive? Was this cop about to realize who they were and storm right back with his gun drawn? Was he calling for backup? Were more cops about to arrive?

"Mom, what do we do?" Jade said, panic in her voice.

"Listen to me very carefully, Jade. We have to run."

"What?" Jade said. "That cop is right there behind us."

"I know. But we don't have a choice."

"Run where?"

"Straight toward the crowd on Sixth Street. And try to get lost."

"What about Dad?"

"When we're in the clear, I'll call him."

Lisa's eyes were locked on her mirror. They needed to get moving while the police officer was still inside his vehicle. That would give them a slight head start. The moment he was out of the vehicle again, they would have a slim chance to get away.

"On the count of three, Jade."

"Mom, this is crazy."

"Do not freeze up on me. Do you understand?"

"Okay, okay. I won't."

"One, two, three—go!"

At that moment, they both opened their doors and jumped out. Lisa made sure Jade moved ahead of her before quickly following. They hopped up on the sidewalk and began sprinting toward Sixth Street. Lisa took a quick peek over her shoulder, almost tripping in the process. The officer was indeed pursuing. Lisa felt more panic surge through her. Jade slowed as they hit the full crowd of Sixth Street, but Lisa just kept shoving her forward.

"Keep going!" she said. "Don't stop until I tell you!"

FORTY-SEVEN

Burns dropped his luggage on the bed inside his downtown hotel room. Davis and Myers had the rooms next door to him on the seventh floor of the Marriott. He planned to take a quick hot shower, get cleaned up, and then huddle again with his team to try to figure out their next move. He'd already been creating a list of individuals he wanted to speak with about their investigation. Many of them were the same people he talked to in the days and weeks immediately after Cole and Lisa's initial disappearance. Family. Friends. Business associates. New information meant new conversations. Burns didn't know why Cole and Lisa had come back to Austin. But he felt there was a decent chance they had intentions to see someone on his list. He needed to both find the Shipleys and figure out what had really happened on the night they'd vanished.

Burns was halfway through undressing when he got a bang on the door.

He hustled over, cracked it open. Agent Davis.

"What?" Burns said.

"I found our leak."

Burns swung the door open. "Come in."

The agent stepped into the room, peeked at his boss in his underwear and undershirt.

"Nice boxers," he said. "No wonder you're not dating again."

"Zip it. What do you got?"

Davis held his digital tablet in his hands. "I carefully back-channeled everything. And I found someone tagging our case who really has no business doing it."

"Who?"

"A guy named Ross Lester."

Burns pitched his head. "I know Lester. He's an old-timer who's been with the Bureau forever. Why do you think he's our leak?"

"Ran his phone, boss. Every time we've logged a new update, Lester has immediately placed a phone call to a lawyer named Carl Fisk."

"Why does that name sound familiar?"

"Because he's a big deal. He's the attorney currently representing Peter Nelson at the Senate confirmation hearings back in DC. According to our records, the calls between Lester and Fisk picked up speed when we left DC for Denver yesterday."

Burns cursed. "Brock Gunner. Peter Nelson. It's all somehow connected."

"That would appear to be the case, sir."

Davis's phone buzzed. He quickly pulled it out, answered it. His eyes widened.

"Where?" he said, and listened. "Text me the exact location."

He hung up, looked at Burns. "Police just found the stolen Ford Explorer. Four blocks from here on Sixth Street. An officer reported a woman and a teenage girl fleeing the scene on foot only a few moments ago."

"Let's get over there!"

FORTY-EIGHT

Jack Harlen was a skinny guy with short black hair, black-rimmed glasses, and surprisingly few tattoos. He wore a short-sleeved blue polo, jeans, and white Converse shoes. In many ways, he looked more like a bank teller than a tattoo artist. He introduced himself and then led Cole down the hallway to a small private studio with huge mirrors on the walls, a counter with all kinds of tools, a fancy black reclining chair, and a black cushioned table.

"Have a seat," Jack said. "What friend did you say recommended me?"

"Marcus Byers," Cole lied.

Jack tilted his head. "Don't remember that name. How long ago?"

"About a year ago."

"What kind of artwork?"

"Picture of his girlfriend. It was uncanny."

Jack laughed. "I do a lot of those. And then I have a lot of repeat customers who come back after they break up hoping I can make something new out of it."

Cole forced his own laugh. "I bet. I hope this doesn't offend you, but you don't look like the stereotypical tattoo artist."

"Yeah, I get that a lot. This is kind of a second career."

"What was the first?"

"Technology startups. Software. Finance. Boring stuff like that. I burned out quickly. Wanted to explore my creative side." He sat on the stool. "So what are you thinking?"

Cole was prepped for this moment. He pulled out his phone, brought up a photograph of Candace McGee, and showed it to him. "Her face on the inside of my left wrist."

The sight of Candace clearly jarred Jack. He jerked back a little in his chair, studied the picture, blinking several times, as if to make sure his eyes were working correctly. Then he brought his eyes from the phone back over to Cole.

"What the hell is this?" he said, his tone darker. "Who are you?"

"Someone searching for the truth. And I need your help."

Jack's eyes narrowed on him more closely. "Wait . . . you're the guy—"

"I'm not dangerous, Jack. I'm someone who's risking everything in order to find out who really killed Candace thirteen years ago. So just be cool, okay?"

Jack calmly turned, opened a drawer below the counter, and pulled out a small handgun. Cole felt his nerves spike. Had this been a huge mistake? To his credit, Jack didn't point the gun at him. He just casually held it in his lap.

"For the record, I'm unarmed," Cole said.

"The FBI is looking for you, right? I've been watching the news."

"I'm innocent, Jack. So is my wife."

"Why're you here?"

"Like I said, I need your help."

"My help? How?"

"Hailey McGee told us you were helping Candace with something at the time of her death. A plan she had to make money and put themselves in a better situation."

"Hailey told you that?"

"Yes, I just spoke with her. Is it true?"

Jack leaned back. "I'm not looking to get into any trouble."

"I understand. But I'm looking to get out of trouble. So if you know something, I'm begging you to help us. If not us, help Candace's daughter."

This seemed to trigger him emotionally. "She is still with you?"

Cole nodded. "She's a wonderful young lady. And she looks a lot like Candace."

Jack swallowed. "I would love to see her, man. How old is she now?"

"She turned fourteen yesterday."

He shook his head. "Wow. That's crazy. I can't believe Candace has been gone that long. I still think about her all the time."

"You two were romantically involved?"

"I wish. I fell in love with her in the eighth grade and never stopped. But she never had any interest in me in that way. No matter what I tried, we were just friends."

"What were you helping her with when she died?"

Jack kind of squirmed in his seat. "She was desperate, man. Her life was a real train wreck. She'd gone through one terrible and abusive relationship after another. She was drinking, doing drugs, stealing things. And then she lost her daughter. But she came to me and said she needed my help to turn her life around. She was going to get sober and help Hailey, too. Apparently, she'd found out that one of the guys she'd slept with—the one who'd gotten her pregnant with Marcy—was some rich guy who was running for office or something. I guess she didn't know it when they'd hooked up, but she saw one of his campaign commercials on TV. Turned out he was also married with two kids. Candace thought she could squeeze him for some cash."

"Do you know who the guy was?"

He shook his head. "She didn't want me to know. She just wanted me to help her figure out how to send an untraceable email, set up a numbered bank account, and then, after the money was wired, help her access it. All of which was easy to do on my end. But I tried to talk her out of it. I told her these things can get messy fast. But like I said, she was so desperate. She came from nothing. So I set it all up for her."

"Did she ever follow through with the plan?"

He shrugged. "I don't know. This was about a month before she died. When she never called me about helping her access the money, I figured she'd come to her senses."

"Did you ever suspect her death could be connected to this plan of hers?"

His brow bunched. "You think it was connected?"

"Yes, I do."

Jack's mouth dropped open, and he slowly leaned back in his chair. "Damn. It honestly never crossed my mind. The police immediately placed all their focus on you and your wife. So it seemed clear from day one what happened to her. Which makes it bizarre sitting here with you right now."

"For me, too. I think Candace tried to squeeze the wrong guy. Someone more powerful and sinister than she ever suspected. And it got her killed. And I think this person is still determined to keep these secrets by sending the same killer after us."

Jack cursed. "You serious?"

"Yes. Is there any way for you to find the email she sent?"

Jack looked uncomfortable. "I don't know, man. I don't want any part of this."

"Please, Jack. Candace is already dead. We can't ever change that. It might have been because of something you unwittingly helped her with. That's not your fault. But if you sit here and do nothing, her daughter might be next. And that's on you."

Jack sighed. "All right, yeah, I mean, I might be able to still access it. If I can still find the platform I used. That was a long time ago."

He slid his stool over to the counter, where he set the gun down and reached for a laptop. After opening it, Jack quickly went to work, typing away, his face close to the screen. Cole took that moment to quickly text Lisa again: You guys still good? He expected to receive an instant thumbs-up reply. But nothing came back. He waited a few seconds more and then texted again: Lisa? Still no response. He stood, moved to the corner of the studio, and called her. The phone rang four times and went to an automated voicemail. He called it again. Same thing. Cole cursed. What was going on? Where were they? Had something happened? He could feel a chill race through him. Something was wrong. He needed to go find them.

"I've got it!" Jack said from across the room.

Cole rushed over. Jack turned the laptop to face him. It showed a sent folder on some obscure private email system with only one message in it.

"You were right, man," Jack said. "She sent this email the morning of her death. I can't believe it. This makes me sick to my stomach."

"Can you open it?"

"I'd rather not see what's in it."

"Okay. Can you download it for me?"

"Yeah, sure." He quickly stuck a tiny thumb drive into his laptop, typed on his keyboard again, and then pulled out the drive. "This will be the only copy. Because I'm deleting this as soon as you leave. If what you're saying is true about the person involved, I have no interest in knowing more. I like my life the way it is."

"I understand. Thanks, Jack."

Cole bolted for the door.

He had to find his family.

FORTY-NINE

Cole was only three steps outside the building, back on the overly crowded sidewalks of Sixth Street, music pumping everywhere, when he suddenly felt a strong hand clutch his left arm from behind. And then a hard pointed object was jabbed squarely into the middle of his back, causing him to grimace. He tried to turn around but was held firmly in place by whoever was behind him. He heard a deep voice at the back of his head.

"No sudden movements. Just walk."

Cole was shoved forward. The object in his back was obviously a gun. Who was behind him? It was clearly not the FBI. They would've identified themselves. The man stayed very close to him, guiding him in and out of sidewalk traffic, never more than a foot away. When they passed the next bar window, Cole took a quick peek over and cursed. The stocky guy. He could see him in the reflection. How was this even possible? How had the guy found them all the way in Austin? Cole was surprised he was not already shot dead. But he knew it was coming soon. The guy was probably just waiting to get clear of the crowd.

Cole felt his heart surge up into his throat. Where were Lisa and Jade? Had this guy already grabbed them? Was that why they didn't answer the phone? The last question in his head almost made him bend over and vomit all over the sidewalk. Could they already be dead?

They kept walking closely together, weaving in and out of the crowds. Cole looked at all the happy faces coming toward him. Could no one tell the guy had a gun pressed against his back? There was no way to alert them with just his eyes. Cole glanced up ahead, spotted two uniformed officers up on police horses. Before, he wanted no part of them. Now he was desperate to somehow grab their attention without getting shot in the process. But the stocky guy seemed to know exactly what was going through his mind.

"Don't be stupid, Cole," the guy whispered into his ear. "Keep walking."

They moved past the police horsemen. They were approaching the end of the building strip at the next street corner. Cole suspected they would be taking a right. And then he'd probably be shoved into an alley and immediately shot. He had to do something. He had to get away. He had to find his wife and daughter. He refused to believe they were already dead. This couldn't be the end for them. As expected, they veered off to the right at the next street. The cross sidewalk was thankfully still crowded. He needed more time to figure something out. Was it possible for him to spin and catch the guy in the stomach with an elbow? Could he somehow knock the gun out like he'd been able to do back in the alley in Winter Park? He had to try. He wasn't going to just stand there and take a bullet.

But then something unexpected happened. Cole heard a loud and hollow thumping sound—like a metal bat hitting a softball—and then the stocky man tumbled forward into him and lost his balance. Cole turned to see what was happening. The guy's eyes had rolled back in his head. He was trying to grab on to Cole to keep from falling. He gripped Cole's hoodie, but he couldn't hold himself up. The gun dropped out of his other hand and hit the sidewalk. Then he let go of Cole's clothing and toppled face-first to the pavement. Cole heard something crack in the guy's face. People around them gasped at the sudden violence. Cole spun around, looked behind him. He was stunned to see Lisa standing there holding a short metal pipe of some sort in her shaky hands. Jade was right behind her. He blew out forcefully. They were alive. They hadn't been apprehended or shot. His wife had just saved him. But how had she known what was happening to him? And why were they in the crowd in the first place? It didn't matter right now. They weren't going to stay alive for long if they didn't immediately get moving. The stocky guy was grunting in pain and already trying to push himself up off the concrete.

"Come on!" Cole yelled at them. "This way!"

Together, they raced forward, away from the stocky guy. They shifted through another group of people before Cole led them into a dirty alley behind the building strip on Sixth Street. It was filled with metal dumpsters, stacks of boxes, trash, and even a few sleeping homeless men. Cole briefly paused to look behind them, searching for the stocky guy, while still yelling at his girls to keep going. How badly was the guy hurt? His skull had taken a beating. Was he still able to pursue them? He got his answer a second later, when the stocky guy suddenly appeared at the end of the alley, stumbling but still moving quickly. Cole spun around, again sprinted forward, his girls just up ahead of him. He then heard the now familiar *thump!* of the guy's gun and ducked his head. He felt nothing. Lisa and Jade were still moving. The guy had missed.

"Keep running!" Cole yelled after his girls.

Jade was in front with Lisa behind her. Cole made sure to stay directly behind Lisa in case more bullets started flying. He would do whatever it took to protect his girls right now. But they had to get away. After everything they'd been through for the past thirteen years, they were so close to potential freedom. He had to believe whatever was in Candace's email—along with the other evidence they had collected— was all they needed to finally prove their innocence. He certainly wanted to get the opportunity.

Another *thump!* rang out, and Cole saw a box directly in front of them explode. A back door from one of the Sixth Street bars opened ahead. A woman stepped out with two trash bags in her hands and walked over toward a dumpster. Cole saw an opportunity.

"Inside the door!" he yelled toward his girls.

They both listened and darted through the open door into what looked like a busy kitchen area. But Cole didn't join them. Instead, he shut the door behind them and took off running again. It was a calculated risk. Left with the choice to follow his wife and daughter into a crowded bar or continue pursuing him, Cole guessed the stocky guy would choose him. He sprinted to the end of the alley, stepped out onto another busy sidewalk, and took a glance back. He'd figured right. The stocky guy remained on his heels. Cole spun back around, darted through a side street, barely avoiding being taken out by a black Camaro. He hit the next sidewalk at full speed, ran south toward Fifth Street. He heard another *thump!* and felt his left earlobe flutter and then start to sting. Had the bullet just hit his ear? Was the shot that close to his head? He had to get off the main sidewalk or the guy would have easy target practice.

He approached a parking garage, hopped over a short concrete wall to get inside, and accelerated up a ramp where cars were stacked up on both sides. Within a couple of seconds, he was out of view from the main level. Cole knew he had a choice to make. Keep running up levels and figure out what to do near the top. Or try to hide and see if he could double back once the stocky guy passed by him. He chose the latter. He would have to hide eventually. He tucked himself in behind a blue Jeep Wrangler with huge mud tires, slid to the floor, and tried to catch his breath. It was difficult. He was panting so hard. Cole reached up, touched his left earlobe, and pulled his hand away. It was covered in blood, which he could now feel dripping down the side of his neck. He had been inches away from death.

Cole held his breath when he suddenly heard shoes sliding on the concrete floor several cars down the ramp. He leaned over and peered out from under the Jeep. The stocky guy. The man had slowed down and was now taking quick glances in between cars as he made his way forward. Cole would have to perfectly time his maneuvering around the front of the Jeep if he didn't want to be spotted. He scooted on his butt toward the very front of the vehicle. The Jeep's large tires were helping block him. But was it enough?

The man with the gun was now directly behind the Jeep. Cole stayed perfectly still. It sounded like the guy had stopped walking. Why? Had he been found? Everything inside him wanted to panic, to jump out from the front of the Jeep, and take off sprinting again. It took all his will to remain patient and be still. It felt like he sat there in silence forever, even though it was only seconds. And then he heard shoes again start sliding forward up the ramp. Two cars away. Three cars. Cole started to breathe again. How far up would the guy travel before turning back around again? He needed to bolt before that happened.

Cole inched his way back around to the side of the Jeep and slowly peeked out. The stocky guy was now ten cars up the ramp with his back to him. Cole returned to the front of the Jeep and, while crouched low, began shifting his way in front of other parked cars down the ramp. He froze in front of a BMW sedan when he heard new footsteps approaching up the ramp. Someone was returning to their vehicle. He scooted back down as to not be seen. But his cover got busted when the BMW's headlights blinked and a man in jeans and a T-shirt slipped in beside the vehicle. At first, the guy didn't see him. But when he opened his driver door, he glanced forward, and they locked eyes.

"What the hell?" the guy immediately blurted out.

Cole was certain it was loud enough to be heard up the ramp. He bolted upright, peered up the row, and cursed out loud. The stocky guy was already racing back in his direction.

"What're you doing by my car, man?" the BMW driver said.

But Cole ignored him, slipped around the passenger side, and took off running down the ramp again. He could hear the killer's shoes slapping hard on the concrete not too far behind him. The guy was relentless. He just never stopped coming. Cole reached the main level and began to make the turn when he suddenly stopped in his tracks.

Another man stood directly in front of him inside the garage. It was Burns, the FBI agent. Burns raised a gun and pointed it directly at him. Cole felt his heart drop and every part of his body tremble. After all this, he wasn't going to be killed by the stocky guy. He was going to be shot dead by the FBI. He instantly thought of Jade. She would not have a father at her college graduation. He wouldn't be there to walk her down the aisle when she got married or hold her child when she began her family. He would never hold Lisa in his arms again and tell her how much he loved her.

But then the agent's gun shifted away from him, and he started firing off his weapon. Several shots. They were loud—unlike the stocky guy's gun with the sound suppressor. Cole turned to look back. He saw the stocky guy stumble to his knees, drop his gun, and then collapse face-first onto the concrete.

A younger and taller FBI agent appeared from around the corner. With his gun also drawn, he rushed forward, past Cole, until he finally reached the stocky guy. The agent kicked the guy fully over with his foot. Looking satisfied that the guy was probably dead, the agent holstered his weapon and pulled out his cell phone. Cole turned back around and noticed Agent Burns had also holstered his weapon. Cole felt his chest violently pumping. He dropped to his knees, his heart racing so fast he thought he might have a heart attack. He started taking deep breaths and letting them out slowly to try to calm down. This was a surreal moment, and his body almost couldn't handle it. It took a moment, but he started to breathe again. He had survived. And he was exactly where he wanted to be right now. With the FBI. With the special agent who had been hunting him down for thirteen long years.

This part of their journey was finally over.

Their next journey would be determined shortly.

Burns stepped up to him. "You all right?"

Cole nodded. Burns offered a hand and helped him up.

"That was a close one," Burns said.

"Yeah. Way too close. Thank you."

"Well, I owed you one."

"Am I under arrest?"

"Not at this very moment."

"Good. I need to go find my family."

"We already have them. They're both okay."

"Thank God." He exhaled heavily. "So what now?"

"We go somewhere safe to talk."

FIFTY

Cole hugged both of his girls tightly, as they all collectively let out a big sigh of relief. Then they were put in the back of a car and taken to a hotel suite nearby. No handcuffs. But no discussion, either. More FBI agents arrived. Four of them waited in the hotel lobby. Two of them stood right outside the hotel suite door. Agent Burns had been on his phone from the moment they'd entered the hotel together twenty minutes ago. Agent Davis got them all bottles of water and then offered to order them room service while they waited—anything they wanted, he said. The FBI's treat. Cole declined. His stomach was still in knots. Lisa asked for a cup of French onion soup. Jade ordered half the menu.

Lisa had explained to him in the car on the way over to the hotel what had happened back on Sixth Street when he couldn't get in touch with them. They had run from the police. And while trying to get lost in the crowd, they'd spotted him and recognized the stocky guy behind him. Lisa said she had reacted on instinct, found the closest weapon available, and swung as hard as she could. Cole was not surprised at his wife's bravery.

He walked over to a window that overlooked Sixth Street. He could see a block of red and blue blinking lights below. Police cars. Ambulances. Fire trucks. They were all surrounding the same parking garage where the stocky guy had met his demise. Cole had felt a massive weight lifted from his shoulders. Having a cold-blooded killer constantly on their tail had been both terrifying and exhausting.

But were there still others? What would happen next?

Lisa stepped up beside him, wrapped her arm around his, and also watched the scene below. "I'm confused. Are they arresting us?"

"Doesn't seem that way, does it?"

"No. So what do you think is going on?"

"I don't know. But I'm eager to put that thumb drive in my pocket into a computer and find out what Candace said in that email. I don't think I'll feel fully confident we're getting out of this nightmare until I do."

He'd already told Lisa about his encounter with Jack Harlen.

"Me too," she agreed. "But it's still so hard to believe how high up this could all go."

Cole turned around when he heard Burns finish his phone call. He watched Burns huddle closely with Davis and another younger agent named Myers, who wore thick black glasses. They were all staring at something on a digital tablet, wide-eyed and shaking their heads. Burns gave Davis some instructions, and the taller agent quickly left the room. Myers returned to a laptop at a table.

Burns finally walked over to them.

"Let's sit down and talk," he said. "We have a lot to discuss."

Cole and Lisa sat on the sofa. Jade squeezed herself in between them. She hadn't wanted to be more than a few feet away from them since they'd been rescued. The past twenty-four hours had been understandably traumatic.

Burns moved to the front of the room and remained standing.

"I'll admit, this is a bit surreal after thirteen years," he began.

"For us, too," Cole replied. "We've dreaded this moment for so long. But we're honestly glad to be in this room with you right now."

"Good. Do you know who that man was in the alley?"

"Sort of," Cole replied. "We know he was the guy at the scene of the crime thirteen years ago. Most likely the one who killed Candace McGee. And the guy you should've been searching for this whole time."

"You're right. And I owe you both an apology."

Cole pitched his head. He was shocked to hear Burns say that.

Burns continued. "But what I still can't understand is why you ran instead of coming to the police or us with the truth."

"We were protecting Jade," Lisa said.

"How?"

Cole went on to explain exactly what Candace had told him that night and why they'd felt like they had no choice but to run—especially after sending the FBI the video through their lawyer had not produced promising results—and continue to hide all these years if they wanted to keep Jade safe and guarantee they stayed together as a family.

"That actually makes sense," Burns admitted. "I have a daughter. She's my whole world, even though she hates me at the moment. I would've probably done the same thing as you. Why were you on Sixth Street tonight?"

Cole told him everything. There was no reason to withhold information now. He wanted it all out on the table. Hailey McGee. The story about being at the bar with her sister and the older, sharply dressed businessman. Finding out about Longshore Ranch and the powerful Nelson family. The supposed plan by Candace to get her and her sister out of poverty. Their suspicion about Peter Nelson being Jade's biological father. Tracking down Jack Harlen on Sixth Street. And then confirming that Candace had really sent an email the morning of her death. Telling the story left Cole breathless in more ways than one. It had been a wild ride. One he never wanted to take again. But he was surprised Burns did not look more shocked.

"You have the email on you?" Burns asked.

Cole pulled the thumb drive out of his pocket, handed it over. Burns walked over and gave it to Myers. The agent stuck it in his laptop and began pecking away. Burns began shaking his head again. He then grabbed the laptop, returned to them, and set it on the coffee table. All three of them leaned forward to read it.

The email included a selfie of Peter Nelson at a bar huddled up closely with what was clearly a young woman, only her face had been completely blotted out with black marker. There was a second photo of Jade as a baby but nothing that identified her. And the final photo was Peter Nelson's law firm business card. One he must've given to Candace, because a personal email and phone number had been scribbled on it.

Cole read the brief email message.

> I saw your political ad. Wife and two kids? It would be a shame if they found out you had another child they knew nothing about. A DNA test would confirm. I also doubt voters would approve of your sexual affairs. I'm prepared to go to the media. But this can all easily go away today. Just click the link below and wire $250,000 to the bank account listed. If you do, I promise you'll never hear from me again. If you don't, I'll destroy you.

Cole exhaled, leaned back, and tried to digest it. The email provided the final piece of the puzzle to prove their innocence. He felt a strange mix of exhilaration and sadness. Two hundred and fifty thousand dollars? That number was pennies for someone like Peter Nelson. And yet he chose death anyway. Poor Candace. She had been so naive.

"Brock Gunner is the dead guy," Burns explained. "He works for the Nelson family. After recovering his phone, we confirmed he's been in constant contact the past twenty-four hours with a burner phone purchased yesterday in Washington, DC—one that we've now directly traced back to Peter Nelson. We have all of their text communication. We have a team already en route to his hotel. He will be charged with conspiracy to commit murder for the events that unfolded the past two days. And we will immediately begin digging to make the case for a conspiracy charge in Candace McGee's death."

Cole shook his head. "If this hadn't happened, Nelson would've been our next Supreme Court Justice."

"We dodged a bullet, thanks to you."

"Well, dodging bullets has been my specialty lately."

"Touché."

"So what happens next for us?" Lisa asked.

"We'll have a long legal battle ahead of us. And we'll require your help."

"Okay, but are we free to go?" Cole asked.

Their entire future hung in the balance of the agent's response to this question.

"Technically, yes. But we'll want to protect you. The ramifications of what is about to happen tonight in DC are beyond explosive. It's going to shake things up for a lot of powerful people. I want to make sure you don't get caught in the cross fire."

"What about Jade?" Cole asked. "Can she stay with us?"

"Yes. I've already talked with Legal. We have some hoops to jump through the next few weeks, but that can all happen while you're together."

Cole was relieved to hear that. It had been a lingering anxiety in the back of his mind ever since they arrived at the hotel.

"Where will you take us?" Lisa asked.

"Somewhere no one else knows about. It'll be nice, don't worry. We keep you there until the dust settles. But I gotta get going myself. The first big domino is about to drop. You guys can stay here tonight. I'll have agents available to get you whatever you need."

Burns and Myers hurried out the hotel suite door, leaving them alone. Sitting there, Cole looked over at Jade and Lisa. Both seemed a little shell-shocked. Just like him. They were free. No more running. No more hiding. No more lies. It felt overwhelming. He had let go of this possibility a long time ago. They both had. Lisa's eyes began to well up with tears. He could feel his own begin to water. It was over. All of it. After thirteen years. They both leaned into Jade, hugging and kissing her, and just held each other for a long time.

FIFTY-ONE

Carl Fisk stood at his office window, expensive bourbon in hand, staring out over the lights of Washington, DC. It was well after midnight. He should be home in bed right now, getting some rest in preparation for a huge day with his client tomorrow in front of the Senate Judiciary Committee. But sleep had been impossible the last two nights. Not with what hung in the balance right now. He'd had some powerful clients create big messes before, but this one took the cake because of everything currently at stake. Like his client, who was sitting in a hotel penthouse suite not too far away, Fisk was eager to get some good news. The kind of news that allowed them both to finally exhale and embrace what tomorrow had in store. If all went well, his client would be confirmed as the next United States Supreme Court Justice by tomorrow afternoon.

But why hadn't they received an update?

Fisk turned when there was a knock at his office door. He was surprised by it. He'd sent his assistant, Brenda, home a half hour ago. Had she returned? He walked over and cracked the door open. He was shocked to see Ross Lester standing there. Same cheap brown suit as always. Same sagging old face and hollow eyes. His FBI insider had been calling him regularly with updates on their dire situation. But why was he suddenly showing up at his office unannounced instead of just calling? This couldn't be good.

"What're you doing here?" Fisk asked.

"I'm going away for a while," Lester said.

Fisk tilted his head. "What the hell do you mean?"

"It's over, Carl. They know."

Fisk's eyes narrowed. "Who knows? What're you talking about?"

"The FBI knows I've been feeding you information. So I've got to disappear."

"Where?"

"Anywhere. Nowhere. It doesn't matter."

"What about your wife?"

"That's probably over, too." He shifted his weight. "But I'm afraid that's not all, old friend."

"What is it?"

"It's over for your client, too. You'd better get over there. In a few minutes, there will be more than twenty FBI agents at his hotel."

Fisk's mouth dropped open. This couldn't be happening. Not when he was this close to having his man sitting in one of the nine most powerful chairs in the world.

"Are you serious?" he said.

"Yeah, they got him, Carl. They got everything. I know you're a good lawyer. But Peter Nelson is done for."

Fisk felt his throat constrict. He had to somehow stop this. He had to work his magic.

"We'll fight like hell," he declared.

"I'm sure you will. But you should worry more about yourself right now."

Fisk felt his heart begin to race. "Am I in trouble here, Ross?"

Lester shrugged. "Who knows. You might be fine. Attorney-client privilege and all that. Can't say for sure. But you should probably prepare yourself. This whole damn town is about to implode."

Fisk cursed, downed the rest of his bourbon in one swig.

"We had a good run, Carl," Lester said. "See ya around."

And then the man in the cheap brown suit left.

FIFTY-TWO

The next day, Cole and his family sat in a small lounge inside a private airplane hangar. In a matter of minutes, they would be leaving the country. Cole had slept so hard last night that Lisa had to shake him awake when room service had arrived with breakfast as the sun rose over Austin. They had all sat there this morning, eating breakfast and watching the breaking morning news on the TV. Every national news station was showing clips of federal agents escorting Peter Nelson from a luxury hotel in handcuffs last night and putting him in the back of a black sedan. It was a stunning sight to behold. Reporters had little information to share at the moment but had been told it would be an absolute bombshell when the FBI held a press conference around noon. Words like *bribery*, *murder*, and *cover-up* were being thrown about on political shows. Nelson's attorney had already been on camera proclaiming his client's innocence, calling it a blatant political attack, and demanding that Nelson be released. Senate confirmation hearings had been canceled for the day. No one seemed to know what was next, but nearly everyone agreed Nelson was likely done for. There was certainly no coming back from this.

"Do you think we're going to the beach?" Jade asked.

Cole shrugged. "Don't know. He just said it would be nice."

Lisa spoke up. "The FBI's version of *nice* could be much different from ours. We could be stuck in a nowhere town in the middle of the desert."

Cole laughed. "That's true. But something tells me Burns is going to take care of us."

"I sure hope it's the beach," Jade said, a huge smile on her face.

None of them had stopped smiling since last night. Cole knew they had some tough days ahead with the expected court proceedings. The case would be explosive and in front of a national audience. But none of that mattered to them right now. For the first time in forever, they were walking in real freedom. No more looking over their shoulders. No more worrying about who might suddenly be knocking on their door. No more lying to Jade. No more living in perpetual fear. They finally had their lives back.

Or, better put, they had a chance at brand-new lives.

"When can we see your family?" Jade asked.

"*Our* family," Lisa corrected.

"Right. It's going to take me a little while to adjust to that thought."

"Soon," Lisa said. "Agent Burns says we can call them once we settle overseas. But it may still be a little while until we can visit them in person."

"I can't wait!" Jade exclaimed. "I feel like I just won the family lottery."

Cole and Lisa shared the biggest grin. They couldn't wait, either. They had missed their families tremendously. Although they had tried to make peace over the years with potentially never seeing them again, if necessary, it had never settled in their hearts.

They suddenly heard a jet landing somewhere outside the hangar. Within minutes, they watched through the lounge windows as a private plane rolled inside the building and came to a stop. A set of stairs was lowered to the concrete and a uniformed pilot appeared.

"Looks like our ride is here," Cole said.

"I can't believe we're flying on a private plane," Jade said. "I feel like a celebrity."

A uniformed woman inside the hangar walked over to the lounge and opened the door for them. "We're ready for you guys."

Jade hurried out of the lounge and raced over to the plane. Cole and Lisa held hands and took their time. He wanted to take his time with everything right now. Jade was already inside the plane when they reached the bottom of the stairs. Cole turned when he heard tires squeal on the concrete and a black Chevrolet Suburban entered the building. When the driver stopped, Agent Burns bounced out the back. He quickly walked over to them.

"Shouldn't you be in DC right now?" Cole said.

"Jumping on a plane right after you guys. Big day ahead. But I wanted to get the chance to see you off. You have everything you need?"

"We think so," Cole said.

"Good. I do have some news I wanted to share with you before you left, because I know it's a big deal. I have contacts in the medical field. I made some calls and just spoke with the most prominent and nationally recognized spine surgeon in the country. He's agreed to take on Jade's case, if you're open to that."

Cole and Lisa shared a stunned look.

"Why would you do something like that?" Cole asked.

"I have a daughter. And I can't imagine having to put her through this kind of surgery. I'd want her in the best hands possible."

Cole nodded. "Thank you."

"Yes, thank you," Lisa added. "This is unexpected and kind of you. Jade will be so relieved."

At that moment, Jade poked her head out the plane door. "Come on, guys! Let's go!"

Burns grinned, reached out his hand. "You better get going."

Cole shook it. "Thank you."

"Likewise. I'll be in touch."

The agent hurried back to the vehicle. They watched as it raced out of the hangar again. Together, they climbed the stairs and entered the plane. There were eight luxury seats. Jade had already claimed hers. A flight attendant met them in the cabin. She said they had plenty of snacks and drinks, and she would serve them lunch once they were in flight. Cole and Lisa dropped into two seats facing their daughter. The stairs were shut behind them and the plane began moving out to the tarmac. All three of them buckled up. Jade was already opening every package in a basket full of snacks and goodies. It was so good to see her happy.

A moment later, they were up in the air. While holding Lisa's hand, Cole watched through the window as Austin gradually disappeared beneath them. He wondered if they would return to Austin, go back to Winter Park, or maybe start over somewhere else.

Would they remain Cole, Lisa, and Jade Shipley?

Or would they go back to Greg, Amy, and Marcy Olsen?

They had *a lot* to sort out.

But all that mattered right now was they were still together as a family.

Cole leaned over, kissed Lisa. She tucked her head into his shoulder.

That's all that had ever mattered.

ABOUT THE AUTHOR

Chad Zunker is the Amazon Charts bestselling author of *The Wife You Know*, *All He Has Left*, and *Family Money*, as well as the David Adams series, including *An Equal Justice*, which was nominated for the 2020 Harper Lee Prize for Legal Fiction; *An Unequal Defense*; and *Runaway Justice*. Chad also penned *The Tracker*, *Shadow Shepherd*, and *Hunt the Lion* in the Sam Callahan series. He studied journalism at the University of Texas, where he was also on the football team. Chad has worked for some of the country's most powerful law firms and has also invented baby products that are sold all over the world. He lives in Austin with his wife, Katie, and their three daughters and is hard at work on his next novel. For more information, visit www.chadzunker.com.